THE SEER

LINDA JOY SINGLETON lives in northern California. She has two grown children and a wonderfully supportive husband who loves to travel with her in search of unusual stories.

Linda Joy Singleton is the author of more than twenty-five books, including the series Regeneration, My Sister the Ghost, Cheer Squad, and, also from Llewellyn, Strange Encounters.

Don't Die Dragonfly

LINDA JOY SINGLETON

flux™

Woodbury, Minnesota

FIRST EDITION
Fifth printing, 2008

Book design and editing by Andrew Karre
Cover design and dragonfly illustration by Lisa Novak
Cover illustration (background) © PhotoDisc

Flux, an imprint of Llewellyn Publications

Library of Congress Cataloging-in-Publication Data
Singleton, Linda Joy,
   Don't die dragonfly / Linda Joy Singleton.—1st ed.
      p. cm. — (The seer; bk. 1)
   Summary: Sabine tries to ignore the psychic abilities that she shares with
her grandmother, but when she discovers that a classmate is in real dan-
ger she is compelled to follow her spirit guide.
   ISBN 0-7387-0526-8
   [1. Psychic ability—Fiction. 2. Supernatural—Fiction. 3. Grandmoth-
ers—Fiction. 4. High schools—Fiction. 5. Schools—Fiction.] I. Title. II.
Do not die dragonfly. III. Series: Singleton, Linda Joy. Seer; bk. 1.
   PZ7.S6177Do 2004
   [Fic]—dc22   2004046577

Flux
Llewellyn Publications
A Division of Llewellyn Worldwide, Ltd.
2143 Wooddale Drive, Dept. 978-0-7387-0526-2
Woodbury, MN 55125-2989, U.S.A.
www.fluxnow.com

Printed in the United States of America

Also by Linda Joy Singleton

The Seer #2, *Last Dance*
The Seer #3 *Witch Ball*
The Seer #4, *Sword Play*
The Seer #5, *Fatal Charm*

Dead Girl Walking

Coming soon by Linda Joy Singleton

Dead Girl Dancing
Dead Girl in Love

To my husband, David, for support, friendship,
and a wonderful life together.

And with a special thanks to my editor, Andrew,
for his help with this book.

WHAT'S UP THIS WEEK

Psychic advice from Mystic Manny Devries

Romantics, listen up! Hold your heart tight. Beware of false promises and fake jewelry.

Green is the lucky color of the week. (Could some unexpected money be coming your way?)

Lucky numbers for this week are 8 and 11.

A kind act will result in many surprising opportunities.

And, to the girl with a dragonfly tattoo, don't do it . . .

FOOTBALL TEAM READY TO RUMBLE

by Vic Wind

Sheridan High's varsity football team began practices yesterday amid rumors about the presence of Pac 10 scouts at the big game with Waindale Central High next month.

TEACHEF

by Dolores Haze

When faced the problem of or brow for two eyes, any sens would reach for tweezers, righ

Apparently not all member: trious staff of Sheridan Valle the same instincts as the stu tain chemistry teacher who nameless is a principal offenc

"I mean, how can I be expec trate on what he's saying ab whatever when there's a cate out on his forehead?" sa Megan Atwood.

Sebastian Knight, a jun that perhaps someone cou creetly slip this teacher a like, maybe he just doesn't l

Other students worry th grooming is an incurable co ondary school faculty, and t not be any hope..

Jerome Dunn said, "At there was this calculus t feet were so bad that we co was coming down the hal utes before he came in th him but he didn't believe really."

When asked about the pal Dunlap knitted his r rated brows but refu

1

"Don't do what?" Manny's beaded dreadlocks rattled as he turned from his computer screen to face me. "Sabine, is this dragonfly girl for real?"

"Of course not." My heart pounded, but I kept my voice calm as I glanced up from the article I was proofreading. School had ended, and except for our teacher, we were the only ones left in the computer lab. "You asked for prediction suggestions and I made up some. If you don't like my ideas, come up with your own."

"It's just a weird thing to say—even for my Mystic Manny column."

"Use it or don't. Whatever." I leaned forward so my blond hair fell, partially concealing my face. If Manny discovered my secret, everything would be ruined.

"Help me here, okay?" He held out his hands. "My column goes to press in thirty minutes."

"Use your psychic powers to figure it out."

"Yeah, right." He snorted. "I don't believe that crap any more than you do."

I gripped my red pencil tightly. "But your readers believe."

"Nah, most of them know it's just a big joke. 'Manny the Mystic knows all and tells all.' Ha! If I could predict the future, you think I'd waste my time at school? No way! I'd pick lottery numbers and predict a sunny future of wealth, women, and tropical beaches."

"Get over yourself already." I checked my watch. "And you have just twenty-seven minutes till deadline."

"Beany, you're one cruel girl."

"Coming from you, I'll take it as a compliment. And don't call me Beany."

"Most girls would be flattered if I gave them a nickname."

"I'm not most girls. And you have twenty-six minutes now." I flipped through last week's edition of the *Sheridan Shout-Out*. My job was copy editor, not columnist. Working on commas and misspelled words suited my new image: helpful and orderly. After my problems at my last school, it was a huge relief to blend in like I was normal. And being on the newspaper made me part of Sheridan High's "In Crowd" without having to reveal much about myself—a great arrangement I wasn't about to risk. Next time Manny asked for help, I'd shout out a big "NO!"

But Manny didn't give up so easily. He pushed his dreads back from his forehead and then scrunched up his face into a pitiful expression. "Come on, Sabine. You have the best ideas. The part about a girl with a dragonfly tattoo—genius. Really, it's a great image—my readers will eat it up. But I can't just say 'Don't do it' without knowing what 'it' is."

It. It. It. The word pounded like a headache and I felt that familiar dizziness. Vivid colors flashed in my head: crimson red swirling with neon black. And I heard a wild flapping of wings. Warning of danger.

Not again, I thought anxiously. I hadn't had a vision since moving to Sheridan Valley, and I'd figured I was through with the weirdness. No longer the freak who knew things before they happened yet had no power to change them.

The dizziness worsened, and I fought for control. Stumbling, I grabbed the edge of a table so I wouldn't fall.

From faraway I heard Manny's voice asking what was wrong, then the lights in the classroom flickered and the drone of computers faded to a distant buzz.

Everything was dark, as if I were swimming in a murky sea at night. Then a light sparked and grew brighter and brighter, taking the shape of a girl. She was stunning, with waves of jet-black hair and olive skin that glistened like sea mist.

She lifted her hand to the sky, and a tiny purple-black

creature with iridescent wings and quivering antennae fluttered to her wrist. A dragonfly. She smiled and caressed the wings. But her smile froze in horror as the creature changed, becoming a fanged monster that sank its sharp teeth into her smooth skin. Blood spurted, swelling like a tide. The girl opened her mouth to cry for help, but there was only a rush of crimson waves, then she sank out of sight.

No, no! I tried to scream. But I was helpless to save her, caught in a dark current of despair that pulled me down, down, into a pool of blood.

*   *   *

"Hey, Beany?"

Gasping for breath, I blinked and saw Manny's black eyes staring at me with concern. The dizziness passed and my head cleared. "Huh?" I murmured.

"Are you sick or something?" he asked.

Lights grew bright again and I realized I was still clutching the table. I relaxed my grip. "I'm fine."

Manny gently touched my shoulder. "You don't look fine. What's wrong?"

"Nothing. Just tired." My breath came fast.

"But you're all trembling."

"Guess that test in calculus wiped me out." I managed a shaky laugh. "I—I just remembered someplace I have to go."

"But Beany—"

"Sorry! Talk to you later."

Then I fled—running as if flocks of winged demons chased after me.

2

By the time I made a sharp left on Lilac Lane, an unpaved, rutted road, the dark images had faded. Still, I was left with a stark fear.

When I slipped through the iron gate of Nona's driveway, my fears eased. The weathered yellow house had been my touchstone since I was little, a haven where nothing could get me. I loved Nona's cozy farmhouse, with its big wraparound porch, rambling red barn, cows, goats, horses, chickens, dogs, and cats.

Ten acres of tangled woods stretched far behind the

pasture, bumping up against new developments. Sheridan Valley used to be a quiet farming town, but its central location made it an easy commute to Stockton or Sacramento and the population had skyrocketed. Still, it maintained a slow pace and country charm, and I'd been truly happy since moving here. Even with upscale houses squeezing in from both sides, Nona's home was my paradise.

And there was Nona. Crouched on her knees in the garden, a wide straw hat shading her deep-lined face. She'd done so much for me: taking me in when my parents sent me away, holding me tight to heal the hidden hurts.

Watching her tend her garden, I longed to rush into her comforting arms. She knew all about visions and predictions. She would understand my anxiety more than anyone. But I couldn't confide in her—because of the lie.

Sighing, I avoided Nona by doubling around to the back of the house. Since there was no one I could talk to, I'd purge my demons with loud music and a bath of scented bubbles.

As I hurried up the wooden steps, chickens squawked out of my way and a white cat with mismatched eyes regarded me solemnly.

"Don't give me that look, Lilybelle. I've had a bad day and I don't need any of your attitude." I patted her silky fur and pushed open the screen door.

There was an odd scent in the air—musty and a little wild. As I made my way through the laundry room and kitchen, I tried to identify the unfamiliar odor. It reminded me of a sunny morning after a summer storm. Fresh, light, but also a little sultry. Had Nona concocted a new herbal carpet freshener? She only used natural cleaners and remedies like crushed pine needle shampoo, goat's milk soap, and a honey rose-petal elixir for sore throats. The smell grew stronger as I walked down the narrow hall, which was decorated with family pictures: Mom as a baby, my parents on their wedding day, and portraits of Nona's three deceased husbands.

A sloshing sound stopped me cold.

From the bathroom. But that wasn't possible. Nona and I lived alone.

I started down the hall, but then doubled back to the kitchen to grab a broom—not that I'd need a weapon, but it wouldn't hurt. Holding it out in front of me like a sword, I moved cautiously down the hall. The bathroom door was open a crack, and through it I could see the sink, filled to the top with water. And perched on the silver faucet was a large bird. A falcon! Why was a falcon taking a bath in my sink?

But the bird wasn't alone.

When I saw the shadowy figure by the hamper, I was so startled I dropped my broom. The bird screeched and ruffled its powerful wings. Before I could scream, the shadowed person lunged for me. He slapped one arm across my shoulders and clamped down over my mouth with the other hand.

"Shush!" he ordered in a harsh whisper. "Don't make a sound."

I struggled, hitting and jabbing with my elbows. But his

grip was firm. He dragged me away from the bathroom. My shock switched to anger. How dare this guy attack me in my own home! I kicked him in leg as hard as I could.

He grunted with pain. "Cut it out!" he cried.

I kicked again, and when he jerked back, his hand over my mouth loosened, so I bit down. Hard.

"HEY! That hurt!"

"Good!" I squirmed and slipped out of his grasp. "I hope I drew blood."

"Geez, you bite worse than a badger." He sucked his injured hand. "Nona was way off when she told me about you."

I backed against a wall. "You know my grandmother?"

"Why else would I be here?"

"You tell me! And what's with the bird?" Hugging myself, I stared, really seeing him for the first time. He was youngish, maybe seventeen or eighteen. He was a few inches taller than I was, maybe five-foot-ten. He was wiry, with muscular arms, sandy-brown hair and eyes like silver-blue mirrors. His jeans were dark, and he wore an unbuttoned, brown flannel shirt over a faded blue T-shirt.

"He's a falcon, and he got oil on his wings, so I brought him inside to clean up. Sorry if I scared you," he said.

"I wasn't scared."

"I didn't want you to startle Dagger." He glanced toward the bathroom where I heard a soft swish of water.

"You *own* a falcon?"

"Wild creatures can't be owned. But he trusts me. If

you'd screamed, he would have panicked and hurt himself. Hey, relax. I'm not going to attack you."

"Oh, thanks," I said sarcastically. "I am so reassured. What do you call what just happened? A friendly hand-shake?"

"Hey, I'm the one bleeding." He held out his hand, where a reddish half circle of teeth marks contrasted his tanned skin. Blood trickled from the deepest mark.

I ignored his hand and gave him a sizzling look. "Explain yourself," I demanded. "What are you doing here?"

"I invited him."

Whirling around, I saw Nona. She still wore her wide-brimmed straw hat and there was a smudge of dirt on her cheek.

"You—you did?" I stammered. "But why?"

"Dominic is going to stay here to help with repairs and care for the animals."

"Why hire someone? I can help you."

"Not in the way he can. So stop scowling and welcome him, Sabine." Nona smiled. "Dominic is part of our family now."

3

After slamming the door to my room, I sorted through my CDs looking for something to match my mood.

If I were at school, I'd listen to the trendy artists everyone raved about. But at home, I could be myself, giving into my secret passion for eclectic music. I indulged in music the same way some people ate certain foods for emotional comfort. Classical for introspective moments, jazz for happy times, and heavy metal for dark, furious moods.

But not even the pounding sound of Metallica and rose-scented bubbles could calm me. How could Nona invite a stranger to live with us without even asking me? It wasn't right! Nona and I had settled into a comfortable routine and got along great. We didn't need anyone else. Not my parents or neighbors—and definitely not some weird guy with a falcon.

I held my breath and sank deep under the warm water.

Stop feeling sorry for yourself, a voice said.

"Go away, Opal," I replied with my thoughts. "I have enough problems."

You don't know how good you have it. When I was your age—

"Not one of your My-Life-Was-Torture stories." I couldn't hold my breath anymore and came up for air. Music vibrated the walls, but the voice in my head came through louder. With my eyes still closed, I could see Opal's critical arched brows and dark eyes. For a spirit guide, she was a terrible nag.

You were rude to that young man, she complained. *Didn't I teach you better manners than that? He's important, you know—or you would know if you listened instead of being so stubborn.*

"Stay out of my head," I told her. "I'm normal now. I have a cool best friend who is even a cheerleader; I'm on the school newspaper staff; and kids like me because I don't hear voices, see spirits, or predict death. No one knows what happened at my other school. I've started over, and I don't want you to interfere."

Whine, whine, whine. You can't run from who you are, so why fight it?

"Go away." I sloshed out of the tub, grabbed a towel, and snapped off the CD.

After I was dressed, I climbed up a curved staircase to my bedroom. It used to be an attic until four months ago when I moved in. Nona had offered me the guestroom next to her office, but I'd begged for the cozy attic room, with its arched ceiling and view of the woods.

Nona also gave me free rein to decorate my room. I chose a lavender theme, draping silky fabric around the windows and arranging daisy-shaped rugs on the polished wood floor. Along with my taste in music, I had "different" taste in hobbies. I'd recently started embroidering a pillow to match my white and purple quilted comforter. I kept my craft materials in a cedar trunk that used to belong to Nona's mother.

Working with my hands always relaxed me, so I slid open the trunk and pulled out the pillow. Using yarn shades from snow white to pale lavender, I'd already embroidered half of the winter landscape picture. At first glance, the soft threads were all white. But as you peered closer, shapes clarified—an owl, a snowman, hills, trees, and a snow-covered cottage.

Weaving my needle in and out, I leaned against the cushion in my window seat and stared across the tops of lush green pines. It was great here at Nona's and I'd never been happier. So why did Nona have to spoil everything by inviting him?

"It's just not right," I complained to my best friend the next day at school. "He's not even friendly. After that whole mess in the bathroom, he's avoided me."

"Maybe he's shy," Penny Lovell—nicknamed Penny-Love—said as she slammed her locker shut. We met every morning at our lockers and caught up on the latest gossip. Bright as sunshine with curly copper-red hair, Penny-Love spun the social wheels around school, and usually did all the talking. But today I had plenty to say.

"His only excuse is a bad attitude. Yet the way Nona treats him, you'd think he was royalty. He doesn't bother coming in to dinner; Nona takes a tray out to him—like she works for him, not the other way around."

"Your grandmother is only being kind."

"This is beyond normal kindness. She gave him the barn apartment, which is bigger than my room and has electricity and a private bathroom. And Nona says she's going to get him a small refrigerator. Can you believe it?"

Penny-Love paused to wave at a group of girls passing by. Then she turned back to me. "Uh, sure. But you haven't told me the important details. Like what he *looks* like."

"He's just weird." I frowned. "There's something strange about him. I can't figure out what exactly; it's just a feeling I have."

Penny-Love giggled. "Maybe you should ask Manny the Mystic for advice. Did you see his column yet?"

"Is it out already?"

"Yeah. And it's better than usual. Here." She unzipped

a pocket of her backpack and withdrew a folded newspaper. "Check it out."

My fingers trembled slightly as I unfolded the paper. A dragonfly with bloody wings flashed in my mind. I shut out the image and focused on the paper.

Penny-Love was right—Manny had outdone himself. He'd added a "spotlight on the future" feature where he picked a random student and predicted her life ten years from now. Sophomore Amanda Redmond was destined to have a great career as a fashion designer, marry an airplane pilot, and have three children—all boys.

Reading over my shoulder, Penny-Love chuckled. "Amanda? A fashion designer? That'll be the day."

"How come?" I asked.

"She wears faded army fatigues and oversized hiking boots. She has zero fashion sense."

I thought Penny-Love was being kind of harsh, but our friendship was still new, so I didn't say anything.

Returning my gaze to the newspaper, I skimmed over the next predictions. Some of them were my suggestions, like the lucky color. Glancing down at the vines embroidered up the leg of my jeans, I hoped green would indeed prove lucky.

When I reached the end of the column and found no mention of the girl with a dragonfly tattoo, I felt relieved—and disappointed. I was glad my silly idea wasn't in print for everyone to see. But I felt uneasy, too, as if I'd let someone down.

"Cool, huh?" Penny-Love said as we reached our homeroom class. "I mean, I don't believe it or whatever, but it's fun. Where does Manny get all his ideas?"

"He has a good imagination. If he doesn't get that Pulitzer he's always talking about, he'll make a great tabloid writer."

"Is that a prediction?" she teased.

"No!" I said a bit too sharply. "I only believe facts."

"Like the fact that you're hot for Josh." She nudged me and pointed to a dark-haired boy as we took our seats. "You ever gonna tell him how you feel?"

My gaze drifted across desktops. The room suddenly felt warm and I couldn't stop staring. Josh DeMarco. Student council junior president, A+ student, a dedicated volunteer, and so fine that my heart sped up just being near him. He was too good to be true—maybe too good for me. And I hadn't found the nerve to talk to him. I probably never would.

The morning went by quickly with a surprise quiz in English lit and extra homework in Spanish. I always ate lunch in the cafeteria with Penny-Love and her group of cheerleading friends, but I'd forgotten my calculus book, so I made a detour to my locker. As I grabbed my book, out of the corner of my eye I glimpsed dark hair and a smile so sweet it took my breath away.

Josh.

Waving as he left his friends Zach and Evan, Josh was walking this way. In seconds, he'd pass by, just inches from me. This was my chance to talk to him, find out if he knew my name and might want to know more. Yeah, like that was going to happen! If I managed to utter one word that would be a miracle.

But I couldn't let him catch me staring, so I leaned closer to my locker—too close! I banged my head on the door, then lost my grip on my book, and it went crashing to the floor. By the time I'd picked it up and shut my locker, Josh had passed.

With a low groan, I watched him pause to talk to a girl with long brown hair, then laugh at something she said before continuing on his way.

Sounds faded and a fog rolled through my mind, clouding everything except Josh. It was as if I was standing next to him, moving in step and sharing his heartbeat. I could even hear this thoughts. He was thinking about his car—a secondhand Honda Civic—and planning to stop by an auto parts store after school to repair a broken taillight. Not paying attention, he walked into his auto shop class. I smelled grease and saw the instructor helping a skinny boy move a car on a lift.

Josh headed straight for a tool cabinet, crouching low to sort through a bottom drawer. He was directly in front of the lift, with his back to it.

My mind was still with Josh as I closed my own locker and began walking towards the auto shop, just at the end of the hallway.

I entered the classroom that was just outside the actual shop. A couple kids noticed me; one was a girl from my calc class.

"Hey, Sabine," she said, but I didn't say anything.

Josh was still hunched over the drawer, looking for something. "Spark plug gapping tool," I heard in my mind. The skinny boy had the control for the lift in his hand now, but the instructor had turned to help someone else.

I was standing in the doorway to the shop, just a few quick strides from Josh. I took a small step toward him.

There was a loud grinding noise and sparks from a machine on the other side of the shop. Josh was still searching. He had no idea. The boy at the lift timidly pushed a green button on the control. The wheels weren't secure; I just knew that. The noise was so loud, but I could somehow hear in Josh's head, "Where is that stupid thing?"

Suddenly, there was a jarring noise and one of the wheels slipped off the platform. The skinny boy frantically pushed the red button, but the car slipped forward. I was now moving in large strides toward Josh. There was so much noise! Running, I reached Josh and pushed him, hard, and we both tumbled over as the car came all the way off the lift and rolled forward, smashing into the tool cabinet where Josh had been standing.

The noise stopped. Josh looked at me. Everyone looked at me.

"Huh?" Josh said in bewilderment. "What just happened?"

Brushing dirt off my jeans, I stood up on shaky legs. I couldn't say anything because all the breath had been knocked out of me.

He smoothed back his dark hair, standing tall so he towered at least a head over me. "Do I know you?" he asked.

"Uh … well … " There goes Miss Conversationalist!

Realization seemed to dawn on him as he looked at the smashed cabinet and the lopsided car. "WOW! That almost hit me! Unbelievable!"

I managed a weak nod.

The instructor rushed over, and, after quickly making sure Josh was okay, he called some students to help move the car.

I started to go, when Josh touched my arm. "Wait."

I waited.

He pushed his hair from his eyes as he studied me. "I don't understand exactly what happened, but I know I owe you a huge thanks."

"Well … " Being near him stole my thoughts.

"How did you know?"

"I—I uh … " I took a deep breath. "I heard the wheels slip."

His dark brows arched. "How could you? It was too noisy to hear anything."

"Everyone says I have unusually good hearing." Did I just say that?

"Lucky for me."

"It's the color green." I pointed at his shirt. "It's lucky."

Josh blinked like he hadn't a clue what I was talking about.

"Don't you read Mystic Manny? He has a weekly column and it's mega popular, so you must have heard about it," I babbled like a fool. Now that I was finally talking to my dream guy, I didn't want it to end.

"Oh, yeah. I know who you mean."

"Then you know Manny writes for the *Sheridan Shout-Out*."

"Oh. The school paper. I was interviewed in it a few weeks ago."

"The September thirteenth issue." I didn't add that I'd clipped the article and tacked it to the bulletin board in my bedroom. I kept right on blathering, "In every issue Manny picks a lucky color and it's green this week. See, I'm even wearing green vines on my jeans."

"Nice design," he said.

Was he checking me out? Did he like what he saw? I was kind of skinny, not much on top, more like a twelve-year-old than a sixteen-year-old. But my face was okay and Penny-Love said my long blond hair was my best feature, that the ribbon of black streaking through my hair was cool. Still, I was unsure. Afraid Josh would take one look at me and run away.

But he wasn't leaving. He was smiling—in a way that made me feel warm inside.

"I've seen you around," he said. "In English."

I stared up into his dark brown eyes and nodded.

"Sabrina?"

"Sabine."

"And I'm Josh."

"I know."

His grin widened into dimples. "Guess I owe you a big thanks. If you didn't have such great hearing, I could have been, like, dead."

"Nah. Only a broken leg or two."

"But I'm all in one piece. I really owe you big-time." He paused. "There must be something I can do to pay you back—"

"No, no! You don't have to—"

"But I want to—want to get to know you."

"Well … that would be cool."

"Are you doing something later this week? Want to see a movie?"

Did I ever! Of course, I didn't say this; instead, I kept my dignity and answered simply, "Sure."

4

A date!

Penny-Love nearly choked on her pompoms when I told her. After school, the other cheerleaders crowded around and wanted to know all the details. I was reluctant to talk so much about myself, not comfortable as the center of attention. But they kept after me, so I gave in and enjoyed the rush of being almost popular. So different than how I was treated at my last school.

And I couldn't wait to tell my grandmother about Josh. Nona was the expert on romance. She ran an online dating service called Soul-Mate Matches. Totally high tech, using compatibility analysis charts and personal videos. Of course, her amazing success rate had little to do with technology— but her clients didn't know that.

Dumping my backpack on the living room floor, I looked for my grandmother. Only she wasn't in the kitchen or her office. The light on her answering machine blinked, as if asking, "Where's Nona?"

Good question.

Heading outside, I checked the garden, chicken pen, and pasture. All that remained was the barn.

I still resented Nona's hiring of Dominic, but not even that could get me down today. I was imagining my grandmother's excited reaction to my news as I peeked into the rambling red barn.

"Nona?" I called out.

No answer, but I caught the scent of burnt lavender. Curious, I pushed open the door. Sunlight cascaded down through a high window, shining gold on stacks of hay. My footsteps on loose hay were soft. A calf, penned for its own safety because it was lame, mooed at the two barn cats who chased each other across a wood rail. I'd always loved this barn, the musty hay smells and all the animals, even the occasional scurrying rat.

My gaze drifted up a staircase, to the loft apartment. The room had been off limits when Nona's last husband was alive and used it as an art studio. I heard the murmur of voices through the closed door—my grandmother and

Dominic. A clunk and a rolling sound piqued my curiosity. So I crept up the stairs. After some hesitation, I reached for the door. At my touch, it fell open a few inches.

My grandmother sat cross-legged on a round carpet across from Dominic. Candles flickered and lavender incense wafted a sweet trail toward the ceiling. Whispering, Nona held out a handful of small stones to Dominic. Sparkling crystals, amethyst, and jade. Stones for meditation and healing. The true tools of Nona's romantic trade.

But why was she showing precious stones to a stranger who'd been hired to repair the barn, feed the animals, and muck out stalls? I felt sick inside, knowing Nona was keeping something from me. A secret was almost the same as a lie. And I knew too well how one lie led to another and another.

Backing away, unnoticed, I fled.

It was childish to feel hurt, left out, like the last kid chosen for a team. But that's how I felt. The happy bubble that I'd floated home in had popped.

I slammed the door behind me as I entered the house, heading for the kitchen, where I poured a glass of milk and ripped open a bag of wheat chips. I had just put the milk away when the phone rang.

Instead of answering right away, I played a childhood game. Closing my eyes and concentrating hard, I tried to summon an image of the caller. Not my parents, I realized with relief. Someone younger, but neither Amy nor Ashley, my nine-year-old twin sisters. Someone older and not related. A dark-haired male…

"OHMYGOD!" I blurted out. I snatched up the phone before the fifth and final ring.

It was Josh, wanting to know if I would mind doubling on Friday with his friend Evan and his latest girlfriend. Yes, yes, yes! Anything you say, Josh.

And with one short, magical phone call, my happy bubble was back. For the rest of the evening, I mentally tuned into a channel where Josh starred in every show. I called Penny-Love and we talked forever, debating what I should wear on Friday and discussing how far to go on a first date.

"It's not like I've never been on a date before," I told her. "Although it'll be my first since moving here."

"Did you have a boyfriend at your old school?"

"A few," I said evasively, not wanting to get on the topic of my past. "Besides, I won't even be alone with Josh on a double date. I'll be lucky to get a kiss goodnight."

Penny-Love then proceeded to tell me in dishy detail about some of her very memorable goodbye kisses. We were still talking when Nona finally came in after dark. My grandmother didn't tell me what she'd been doing, and I didn't tell her about Josh.

When I got ready for bed, I chose a heart-shaped nightlight and hoped for sweet dreams of Josh. The dark had always scared me; so, childish as it was, I never slept without a nightlight. This led to a huge nightlight collection. Plug-in lights shaped like kittens, dolphins, rainbows, angels, butterflies, and a stained-glass flaming dragon.

Instead of hearts, though, I dreamed of dragons. Dragons chasing after me, blowing molten fire, their razor teeth white knives of death. I ran and ran, calling out to Josh to rescue me. And there he was, tall and handsome, grasping my hand. He protected me with a silver shield, dodging bursts of flame. We raced through a maze of spindly spines that became a giant dragon.

There was a loud flapping, and the dragon sprouted wings. Josh slipped and started to fall, only I lunged forward and grasped his hand. Holding on tight, we clung together as the dragon flew higher, higher, soaring into the unknown. Then the dragon changed, spines smoothing into silky feathers and fangs curving into a sharp beak. Soaring along on a strong breeze, we rode the giant bird. A falcon. When I looked at Josh, he was different, too. His dark hair grew longer and lighter, to a sandy brown, and his eyes shone as blue as the sky. Dominic...

I sat bolt up in bed.

My heart revved and my hands were sweaty. Despite my nightlight's reassuring glow, the shadows around my room moved and breathed, and I sensed I wasn't alone.

I was never alone.

Climbing out of bed, I walked over to the wall and snapped on the light.

Then I slipped back under my covers and sank into a fitful, dreamless sleep.

*   *   *

The next morning when I went to my locker to meet Penny-Love, instead I found Josh. And this was only the beginning of a perfect day.

Just like that, I was Josh's girl. Instead of sitting with the cheerleaders at lunch, Josh and I sat outside under a willow tree, sharing sandwiches and chips and talking. Mostly, I listened while he described his interest in magic. Not the kind of magic I'd avoided all my life, but entertaining magic tricks.

He was apprenticing to join a professional magician's organization. So secret, he couldn't reveal much, except that only the most respected, skilled magicians belonged. And his mentor, the Amazing Arturo, was rumored to be a distant cousin of Houdini.

"How'd you get interested in magic?" I asked, impressed that a popular guy like Josh had such an unusual hobby.

"Arty—the Amazing Arturo—showed me some tricks and I was hooked."

"How long have you known him?"

"Seven years." Josh hesitated, taking a sip of cola. "We met at Valley General Hospital where he was giving a show in the children's ward."

"What were doing you there? Were you sick?"

"Not me. My older brother." His tone had grown serious.

"What was wrong with him?"

"A car accident. He was in a coma for five months."

"I'm sorry. How is he now?"

"He didn't make it." Josh spoke calmly but I sensed deep loss and I regretted asking the question. "It's been a long time," he quickly added. "And because Arty noticed me hanging around the hospital with nothing to do, one thing led to another, and now I'm the one performing for sick kids."

"That's great of you."

"It's the kids who are great. And it's so cool to amaze them. Wait till you see my latest sleight-of-hand trick. You'll never guess how it's done."

"I wouldn't even try. I'd rather be mystified."

"Then you gotta watch me the next time I perform at the hospital. Will you come?"

"I'd love to." And I loved staring at his face, his soft lips, straight nose, and long, dark lashes. He was so perfect. And he liked me. Amazing.

Penny-Love came over that night, just one day from The Date, and searched through my closet for the right outfit. Unfortunately, all my clothes were wrong. So I broke down and admitted to my grandmother why I needed a new outfit. She had a million questions about Josh, and was impressed when I told her about his volunteer work. Always a fan of romance, Nona gave me encouragement—and her credit card—then told me to have fun shopping.

We headed for Arden Fair Mall in Sacramento, about thirty miles away. Penny-Love borrowed a station wagon from one of her older brothers. Nick or Jeff or Dan—with a family as large as hers, all redheads with freckles, who could keep them straight?

The perfect outfit was a dark-green skirt with a yellow Lyrca top. Penny-Love talked me into buying one of those pushup bras, which made me blush when I looked in the mirror. For the first time in my life, I had curves in the right places.

*   *   *

When Friday night arrived, I breathlessly watched Josh walk up to my front door. I didn't need to be psychic to know my outfit was working a subtle magic. This was my moment and nothing could spoil it. Not even Dominic, whom I saw standing in the shadow of the porch, scowling as Josh opened his car door for me. What was his problem anyway? He'd barely spoken two sentences to me since we'd met, yet I had the weird feeling he disapproved of my going out.

"You look great," Josh said as we drove off to pick up his friends.

My cheeks warmed. "Uh … thanks."

"I'm glad you don't mind doubling with Evan and Danielle."

"It'll be fun." I smiled.

He smiled back.

I could tell he liked me, but then when I thought about it, I wasn't sure and wondered why a great guy like him would even notice me. Sure I'd rescued him, yet gratitude wasn't any basis for a relationship. We'd gotten along great so far, but would that change if he knew the truth about me?

There was an awkward stretch of quiet, and I tried to think of something interesting to say. I had to be careful not to reveal too much, yet I didn't want to bore him with topics like weather or homework.

Then I remembered some advice I'd heard Nona give

to one of her clients. When in doubt about what to say, ask your date about himself.

"So Josh," I said, "tell me about yourself."

"What?"

"Anything." I shrugged. "Like do you have a pet?"

"A dog named Reginald."

"Do you call him Reggie for short?"

"Nothing short about my giant dog. We nicknamed him Horse."

I laughed. "What's your family like?"

"They're great. Mom's a Realtor and Dad has some kind of management job at EDH Compu-Tech. They're always busy, so we have this terrific housekeeper who makes the best lasagna."

"Oooh. My favorite," I said, smacking my lips. "I used to make it for my little sisters."

"How old are they?"

"Nine."

"Both of them?"

"Amy and Ashley are twins," I explained. Then, because I suspected he was thinking of his brother, I purposely switched the subject and asked him about the couple who would be joining us soon.

"Evan and I have been friends since we were babies, practically," Josh said as he slowed for a stop sign. "He's a year older, and a fantastic athlete. Football, wrestling, baseball—you name it, he's good enough to go pro. As for Danielle, I only know what Evan's told me, that she's smart and pretty. Evan dates a lot so it's hard to keep up."

"Do you date a lot, too?" I asked, then wanted to slap my hand over my mouth.

"Hardly ever," he said firmly. "Evan's fixed me up a few times, but it never works out. He says I'm too picky. But I only want to be with someone I respect."

He took his right hand off the steering wheel, resting it inches from my arm. I could feel his energy without even touching, and it made me a little dizzy. In a good way.

Then we were slowing and parking in front of a ranch-style home. Two figures came down the steps. I recognized Evan's cocky grin and wide, muscular shoulders from the sports section of the *Sheridan Shout-Out*. His arm was draped around the tiny waist of a slim, raven-haired girl. While he moved with confident strides, she sort of glided like a shadow beside him. She looked familiar, although she wasn't in any of my classes, and I was sure we hadn't met before. The feeling of knowing her was strong, so I turned around for a better look.

Danielle flashed me a nervous smile as she climbed into the backseat with Evan. She had an exotic sort of beauty—smooth olive skin, a nose that was a bit long, and high cheekbones. Her strapless navy-blue sheer top showed off ample curves that didn't need any extra help. I felt a stab of envy, wishing looking good came so easily to me.

Then I noticed the dark tattoo on her wrist.

A tiny outline of a winged insect.

A dragonfly tattoo.

5

I swallowed the lump in my throat and tasted fear. Shivering, I couldn't take my eyes off the dragonfly tattoo. Its wings fluttered and my head swam dizzily. There was a hammering sound, a heart beating—Danielle's heart. And I saw the horrific image of her heart soaring through her chest into the air, suspended by wings. The wings flapped wildly, pulling in opposite directions, until the heart split apart.

"Sabine? What's wrong?" I heard someone ask.

"Huh?" I shook away the weird images, and fought to stay sane. The dizziness passed and I was aware of Britney

Spears on the radio and the hum of the car engine. Josh and Even were talking to each other, something about football. And Danielle was leaning toward me with a confused expression.

"Why were you staring at me like that?" Danielle asked, her voice soft like a little girl's. "Is my hair messed up or something?"

"Your hair is fine."

"Not too frizzy?"

"You look great. I—I was just admiring your tattoo."

"Oh, that." She sounded relieved.

"A dragonfly." I paused. "It's really … really unique."

"Thanks! My grandmother was an artist and I had it copied from an old sketchbook of hers. She's gone now, but it's like part of her is with me always." She glanced at Evan who had leaned back and was smiling at her. "My next tattoo is gonna be for Evan. We could even get matching heart tattoos."

"Hearts?" I repeated, cringing a little.

"Or maybe our initials."

"As long as you don't ask me to pierce my nose or lips," Evan told her. "I don't want to look like a freak. Besides, I know a better way of showing you how I feel."

Suddenly embarrassed and feeling like a peeping Tom, I turned around and looked straight ahead. Agreeing to a double date suddenly seemed like a terrible idea. And I couldn't shake that sense of fear. How could I warn Danielle about some unknown danger without revealing my gift?

Why didn't my visions come with a how-to book? If I told Danielle I was psychic, she'd think I was crazy. Worse—she might tell Josh and he'd drop me quicker than yesterday's garbage.

But when I ignored visions, bad things happened. I knew from experience—terrible experience—how real they could be.

What am I going do to? I thought desperately. How can I help Danielle without hurting myself? Of course there was no answer. When it came to predicting my own future, I always came up with a blank screen.

I glanced over at Josh and caught him studying me. "You okay?" he whispered.

"Never better," I lied, ignoring the slurping noises coming from the backseat. "What movie are we going to see?"

"Evan likes the new Will Smith movie. But if you'd rather see something else—"

"No, that sounds good."

"Great," he said. "I told Evan we should check with you before picking the show, but he insisted everyone likes this movie, and he knows more about movies than I do. Still, next time you can pick the movie."

Next time. I'd never heard more wonderful words. And I resolved to forget about crazy visions, and enjoy my time with Josh.

When we got to the cinema complex in Lodi, Evan wanted to sit in the far back, so that's where we headed. He wanted an aisle seat, so Josh and I moved over. I was beginning to notice a pattern in Evan's attitude—it was his way all the time. Josh was so easygoing, he didn't seem to mind. And Danielle was crazy for Evan, clinging to him like lint. She seemed much more serious about their relationship than Evan.

Warn her, Opal's voice popped into my head.

"Leave me alone," I thought.

You have to stop her before it's too late.

"Go away!"

I realized I'd spoken aloud when Josh set down the soda he'd been sipping and looked at me with surprise. "You want me to go?"

"No. Not you. I mean—" I hesitated, aware that Evan and Danielle were giving me odd looks, too. The movie hadn't started yet, so I stood and added, "I—I meant I have to go ... to the restroom."

Danielle stood up. "Me, too."

"Can't girls go anywhere alone?" Evan joked. "Josh, you notice how they always travel in packs. At school, to the mall, and to the bathroom."

"It's so we can talk about you," I couldn't resist saying.

"Talk all you want," Evan said. "As long as it's good."

"Only the best." Danielle bent down to kiss him. "I'll hurry back."

"You'd better or I'll eat your half of the popcorn." He grabbed a handful of popcorn and shoved it into his mouth.

I turned away quickly. A little bit of Evan went a long way.

"Have you and Evan been going out long?" I asked Danielle as we entered the restroom.

"Three weeks, two days, and six hours." She set her purse on the counter in front of the mirror and pulled out lipstick, mascara, and a brush. "But it feels like forever. I never thought a cool guy like him would notice me. I've usually too busy studying and don't have many friends. But now I just want to be with Evan all the time. Is that how it is with you and Josh?"

I felt my cheeks heat up. "This is our first date. I hardly know him."

"But it's obvious you really like him."

"Well...yeah."

"And he really, really likes you. Evan says Josh is super-picky about girls and hasn't dated since last summer. I have a real good feeling about you two."

"Do you trust your feelings?" I asked cautiously.

She shrugged. "I guess."

We stood in front of the mirror, and I searched past her striking beauty for her aura. Faint colors of green and orange swirled in opaque gray. Whatever that meant! Opal was good about telling me what to do, but she was terrible about explaining things.

My gaze locked on Danielle's tattoo, and I found myself saying, "Danielle, are you in any trouble?"

"Trouble?" She set down her brush and gave me a wide-eyed look. "Why do you ask? I've got Evan and everything is great."

"Yeah, but... see, I—I had this dream. And you were in it."

"Really?" She giggled a little nervously. "Was Evan in it, too?"

"This isn't about him. It's about you." I hesitated, getting that old sinking feeling, the same one I had right before I was kicked out of my last school, when I'd looked at a popular football player and saw his face burning down to a skull and heard sounds of a car crash. When I'd warned him not to drive after the prom, he'd spread the word that I was a freak. Everyone laughed at me. But when he drank too much on prom night and died in a head-on collision with a truck, nobody laughed anymore. They were afraid. Of me.

"Tell me about your dream while I fix my hair," Danielle said. "But make it quick. Evan gets in a bad mood if I make him wait."

"Dreams aren't important. I shouldn't have even brought it up."

"But it's an amazing coincidence you dreamed about me before we even met."

"Nothing amazing about it. I've probably seen you around school. And I knew I'd be meeting you tonight."

"I help out in the school office, so you could have seen me there. "

"Yeah, that must be it. We better hurry or you won't have any popcorn left." I glanced at my reflection in the mirror, not sure I liked what I saw, then quickly turned away and followed Danielle.

The movie must have been hilarious because the audience roared with laughter, but it was impossible to notice anything other than Josh's hand holding mine.

Josh drove Evan and Danielle to Evan's house. Then we were alone.

Parking in front of Nona's driveway, Josh turned off the engine but made no move to get out of the car. Instead, we sat silently for a moment in the darkness. Moonlight shifted through nearby trees and shone golden on Josh's face. I found myself thinking about kissing, hoping Josh wanted to. I held my breath as I unsnapped my seat belt. It slid off my shoulders with a metallic click.

"Sabine—" He cleared his throat.

"Yes?" I said too quickly

He smiled. "I had a great time." He held out his hand.

"Me, too." I clasped his gentle fingers.

"I don't want you to go in."

"All right." My mouth was moving but my brain had thrown in the towel. I was numb.

He grinned. "Your parents wouldn't like that."

"My parents live in San Jose. I stay here with my grandmother."

"Really? But don't your parents miss you?"

"I don't think so."

"It's their loss." Then he leaned forward, pulled me close, and kissed me.

6

Saturday morning, I awoke to a crowing rooster. It was tempting to lie in bed a little longer, thinking of Josh, reliving his kiss, but I had chores to do. So I slipped into my grubbiest clothes and went on a treasure hunt.

Inhaling the crisp air, I picked a trail through dewy grass. Nona's cow, Daphne, mooed from the pasture and a meadowlark chimed in with a cheerful song. Even though I'd been living with Nona for nearly four months, I had one of those "Ohmygod, I can't believe I'm here," culture-shock moments. I expected to hear arguing neighbors or traffic whizzing by with honking horns. But at Nona's farm, the only honking came from flocks of geese. No noisy little sisters bugging me, hammering on their many musical instruments, showing off their talents. And I didn't have to face the condemning stares from classmates, teachers—even my own mother. Living with Nona was a new start.

Entering the chicken coop, I made my way through dirt, feathers, and chicken poop. The first eight eggs were easy to find lying on the ground. One, two, three more tucked in a nest of weeds. But some hens hid their eggs carefully, and it took at least ten minutes before I finally spotted a speckled green egg tucked under a dark corner of the coop. Crawling on my knees, I reached out for the still-warm egg. A gentle nudge and my prize rolled close.

"An even dozen," I murmured triumphantly, adding the egg to my basket.

"Why not go for a baker's dozen?"

Dominic stood outside the chicken coop with his arms folded across his chest. His falcon wasn't around, probably soaring over the woods in search of breakfast. "You missed one," he said in a mocking tone.

"Oh yeah?"

"Look under that bush." He pointed to a prickly berry bush with tangled and barbed vines twining through the fence.

"Forget it." I shook my head. "That's too thorny even for the chickens."

"Never underestimate an animal. It's a large egg, too."

"How do you know? You can't possibly see a tiny egg through all those vines."

"A little bird told me."

"Yeah. Right." I rolled my eyes but couldn't resist a challenge. Cautiously, I pulled the vines aside and peered into the bushes. "Nothing there."

"It's toward the left. Yeah, you should be touching it now."

As he said "now," my hand closed around a smooth egg.

Instead of being grateful, I wanted to slap the smug smirk off his face. Only when I looked up, ready to tell him off, I saw a woman hovering beside him.

She was part sunshine and part fog. Short dark hair curled above her neck and smile lines crinkled around her shining black eyes. I knew without being told that Dominic had called this woman "Mom."

"What are you staring at?" Dominic demanded sharply.

"Can't you see?" I asked in a trembling whisper.

"See what?"

"Her." The woman reached out to Dominic, surrounding him with love as sweet as a summer breeze.

"There's no one here except us. " Dominic furrowed his brow, looking around with a puzzled expression.

I shook my head, realizing too late that I was the only one weird enough to see ghosts. It hadn't happened like this since moving in with Nona. Even the night shadows and the voices had quieted down. But I should have known it wouldn't last. I was cursed, an unwilling messenger for spirits. Once again, the other world was bleeding into my own.

My darling Nicky, I heard the woman say.

"Who's Nicky?" I asked.

Dominic's mouth fell open. "No one's called me that since I was young. Since my mother—"

"Died," I finished.

I left my son too soon. Couldn't help when he needed me. She held out wispy arms in an imploring gesture. I felt her emotions: love, loss, and longing. *Tell him 'A nickel for your thoughts.'*

"A nickel for your thoughts?" I repeated in confusion. "Isn't that saying supposed to be 'A penny for your thoughts?'"

The color had faded from Dominic's face. He lunged forward, grabbing my arms. "What kind of game are you playing?"

"Nothing." I shook him off. "And don't you ever grab me again!"

His shoulders sagged. "Sorry. But my mother always said 'nickel' because of my name. No one else knew that. How did you?"

I shook my head, overwhelmed with emotions as I watched a tear fall from his mother's misty face. She lifted her hand to show a silver coin glittering in her palm. A nickel. Reaching out with filmy fingers, she tucked the nickel in Dominic's pocket. Her body began to fade until all that was left were bright blue eyes. Then they rose high like ascending stars, blending blue into sky.

And she was gone.

Dominic looked at me with disbelief. "What are you seeing?"

"Nothing," I answered truthfully.

"Then why did you say that stuff? Did someone tell you about my mom?"

"No. I don't know anything." I hugged my basket to my chest, glancing down at the eggs. "I—I have to go."

He stepped in front of me. "Not until you explain what just happened."

"I can't. I never can." Then clutching the basket to my pounding chest, I pushed past him.

The door to the house banged behind me as I entered the kitchen. Setting the basket on the tile counter, I bent over to catch my breath. What *had* just happened? Why had Dominic's mother appeared to me? Had she been using me to visit her son one last time? Or had she come to warn of danger?

I shuddered, remembering that fatal prom night. I'd known the boy was going to die, yet could do nothing to save him.

As I placed the eggs in an egg carton, I wondered if I should go to Nona and confess everything. She'd know how to help. She often told me how we'd come from a long line of psychics. It had skipped a generation with my mother, but Nona was certain I'd inherited the family "gift," that the black streak through my blond hair was the mark of a Seer. She'd offered to nurture my abilities, but I didn't want to be different. I wanted to be an ordinary person who didn't see ghosts or know things before they happened. Besides, I could never be certain whether I was predicting tragedies or causing them.

So I'd lied to Nona, insisting that I'd outgrown my "gift." It took some convincing, but she eventually believed me. If I told her the truth now, she'd never trust me again, and she'd be deeply hurt.

I couldn't bear that.

So I whispered a plea to my spirit guide to make all the weirdness go away. Then I took the cordless phone into my room and shut the door.

I wanted to talk to Josh, but knew he was busy with his family this weekend. Instead, I made my weekly calls home, which felt wonderfully normal. I had a quick talk with Dad who could be found at his office even on Saturday. Then I made a call to my sisters—Ashley was out with friends, so I talked to Amy. She had a collection of vintage girl series books and described the entire plot of her newest addition, a dust-jacketed copy of *Swamp Island Mystery*. She was explaining how the author also wrote some original Nancy Drews when I heard my mother's voice in the background. But I didn't ask to speak to her, nor did she ask to speak to me. There was nothing to say.

I'd barely hung up when Penny-Love called, wanting to know all about my date with Josh. I was delighted to tell her. I was describing "the kiss" in delicious detail, when Penny-Love had a call waiting beep and left me on hold.

Seconds later, she came back, apologetic because she had to go to a cheer practice.

"We'll talk later," she promised.

"Not till Monday," I complained. "You're always so busy."

"So come with me to the cheer club meeting tomorrow night at Jill's house."

"But I'm not a cheerleader."

"When did that ever matter? You're practically part of the squad, like a mascot."

"I've seen the mascot costumes—and no way am I dressing up like a shark."

"You have a point." Penny-Love laughed. "The costumes are really lame. Lucky for you, there's no costume required to hang with us. And you're so artistic, the group will be thrilled to have your help. Say you'll come."

"Okay, okay." I laughed at her. "I'll come."

After hanging up, I wandered into the kitchen for a snack. I'd skipped breakfast and it was past time for lunch. A PLT—pickle, lettuce, and tomato—sandwich sounded good. Or maybe some clam chowder?

While I tried to decide, I noticed the egg carton where I left it on the counter. I'd meant to put it in the refrigerator. I started to pick it up when I heard a crash from the back of the house.

Worried about Nona, I set the carton down and ran out of the kitchen. When I entered my grandmother's office, I found her digging through her closet, with her rear stuck up in the air.

"Nona, are you okay?" I asked, coming up beside her.

"Yes. This is just so frustrating!" My grandmother tossed a box on the floor beside me and swore under her breath.

"What?"

"I can't find the notebook where I wrote down my computer password." She shuffled through a folder, then tossed that aside, too.

"Don't you know the password by memory?"

"I did until yesterday when I updated my computer and changed the password. Then I wrote it down in a blue notebook, just in case I forgot."

"And you forgot?"

"I thought it was 'cupid,' but that turned out to be an old password. So I tried 'sonnet,' 'valentine,' and 'sweetheart.' None worked! Where did I put my notebook?" She sank wearily into her swivel desk chair. "I even consulted my crystals and the tarot, but that didn't help either."

"You don't need the other side, Nona. I'm here for you."

"Thanks, sweetie. All my client information is on my computer. I'm ruined if I can't access my files. I know I put the notebook in a safe, dark place where I wouldn't lose it— only now I have."

I patted her arm reassuringly. "We'll find it."

But after checking every folder, drawer, shelf, and scrap of paper, we didn't.

I was ready to go against everything I believed in—or

didn't want to believe in—and ask Opal for help. But before I got a chance, Nona suggested we put the search on hold and have lunch. When we entered the kitchen, I spotted the egg carton still on the counter where I'd left it.

"You're not the only one who forgets things," I told my grandmother with a wry smile. "I better put it away."

I pulled open the refrigerator door. Then I stared in astonishment. I couldn't help myself—I started laughing.

"What is it?" Nona demanded.

"Look!" I pointed inside the refrigerator where a blue spiral-bound book was propped between a blueberry jam jar and a catsup bottle.

I'd found Nona's missing notebook.

7

Shake it, shake it, rattle and roll.

Win, win, win! That's our goal.

Penny-Love and Jill jumped high, waving their poms, then slid down in perfect splits.

"That was great!" I said, applauding from the garage floor where I was on my knees painting a large letter *H* in shades of red, white, and blue on a poster. Adding a patriotic theme was my idea, and I was glad the others approved.

Jill's house was in a subdivision near the school, about a

mile from Nona's farmhouse. Since we were having a mild October, I'd walked over instead of driving.

I enjoyed hanging out with such energetic, hard-working girls. Cheerleaders weren't the fluff-brains I used to think, but seriously dedicated athletes. I admired that, but no way did I want to wave poms or do the splits in front of crowds. Watching from the sidelines suited me fine.

Four members of the Sheridan Spirit Squad were present: Penny-Love, Jill, Catelynn, and Kaitlyn. They all wore sweats and T-shirts, except for Penny-Love who never dressed down, not even when she planned to paint. She'd twisted her wild red hair into twin French braids and wore a high-cut purple stretch top that showed off the diamond pierced into her bellybutton.

"You're a great audience, Sabine," Jill said with a flash of her pearly smile. She was team captain and brilliant at creating new routines. "It still needs work, but we can practice later. It's more important to finish the posters."

"This one's almost done." I said as I dipped my brush into the red paint and filled in the outline of the letter *H*.

"I got more paint on myself than the poster," Catelynn complained as she held out a long strand of her blue-splattered brunette hair. "I'm a disgusting mess."

"That for sure," her best friend Kaitlyn teased. Although Catelynn and Kaitlyn shared a name, they were total opposites. Perfectionist Catelynn was often critical, while Kaitlyn had a kooky sense of humor.

"We're all a mess, but it'll wash off," Jill said.

"But Catelynn is the worst," Kaitlyn pointed out. "She looks like a rainbow exploded on her."

Jill giggled. "True. Catelynn, you even have paint in your ears."

"Anyone got a camera?" Penny-Love asked. "This would make a great front-page shot for the *Shout-Out.*"

"Or I could give Manny a call—among his many duties, he's also the staff photographer," I said.

"Don't you dare!" Catelynn protested. "Or I'll wipe paint all over you."

"Okay, okay," Kaitlyn said with a giggle. "Truce."

"I was just kidding," I added. "I wouldn't really call Manny."

"Too bad," Jill said with a sigh. "Oh-So-Fine Manny is welcome here anytime."

"I just love his column," Kaitlyn added. "He did a great job on that ten-year-in-the-future article. I'd love for him to write about my future."

I smiled, used to these sort of comments by now. Manny didn't care what anyone thought of him, dressed and acted exactly as he pleased, and instead of being an outsider, he got respect.

"I chose these earrings because Mystic Manny says green is lucky this week." Jill pointed to her jade earrings.

Kaitlyn grinned. "I wouldn't mind getting lucky with him."

"He's too full of himself for my taste." Penny-Love wiped her nose, leaving a streak of green paint. "Sabine's the lucky one. She's got the coolest guy at school drooling for her. Guess who she went out with Friday night?"

"Josh DeMarco. You already told us, Pen," Jill said, rolling her eyes. "And they doubled with Evan and his latest."

"Her name's Danielle," I said with a prickle of anxiety.

"Don't know the girl." Catelynn gave a dismissive shrug. "And the way Evan Marshall jumps from one girl to another, she won't last long anyway."

"I hope you're wrong." The anxious feeling grew, stabbing like needles. "Danielle is very sweet and terribly in love. I'd hate to see her hurt."

"It's gonna happen," Catelynn said as she wiped paint off her hands with a rag. "Face it, Sabine. You haven't gone to Sheridan long enough to know about Evan Marshall, but we know how he works. He's a player. 'Moving On Marsh' they call him."

"That's terrible."

"At least you've got nothing to worry about with Josh," Penny-Love assured. "He's as good as they come."

"So why does he hang around a jerk like Evan?"

"Because their parents have been friends forever and they live next door to each other," Penny-Love explained. "Evan runs over people like a bulldozer, but Josh doesn't seem to notice."

"I noticed," I said, remembering how Evan made all the decisions on our date. And he hadn't seemed very friendly to me, either, like I wasn't important.

"Josh can only see the good side of people," Penny-Love

continued. "He's always volunteering for charities and helping out on school committees. He's kind of idealistic, wanting to help people and change the world."

"No one can do that," Catelynn said with a skeptical sniff.

I wanted to argue with Catelynn, except I was afraid she was right.

My head throbbed, and the rainbow I was painting blurred. A wave of dizziness swelled over me, and I doubled over in agony. The brush slipped from my fingers as swirling paint came alive, circling around me, wings flapping. I saw a vivid image of a dragonfly fluttering out of Jill's house, down the street, zooming into Sheridan High and disappearing into a dark-red pool of blood.

Danger.

Hurry.

My heart sped up and fear filled my throat like bile.

I wanted to ignore this vision, but even with my eyes open, the bloody dragonfly fluttered in warning. I had no idea what I was supposed to do; I just knew that if I did nothing, something terrible would happen.

To Danielle.

8

It was insane to rush off without even taking the time to wash the paint from my hands, making up an excuse so dumb they must all think I'm crazy. But if I could help someone this time, maybe that would make up for past mistakes. I had to try at least.

Clouds had blown in, darkening the dusk sky, giving me shivers. I'd forgotten how early night fell this time of year. The deserted sidewalk was only partly lit up by an occasional street lamp. When I reached the entrance to Sheridan High, I hesitated, afraid to leave the safety of the street. But I did it anyway, and I started across the schoolyard. A single yellow light illuminated the entrance, casting dark shadows.

If I'd stopped to think, I would have realized all the reasons why I shouldn't be doing this. I was trespassing. I had no actual proof that Danielle was in trouble. Even if she were, how could I help her? I tried to think of some skill I had that might be useful if I had to defend Danielle or myself. I'd taken fencing lessons at my last school, but I didn't exactly carry a foil around in my backpack.

The vision of a bloody dragonfly pushed me forward, urging me to rattle locked doors until I found one that was open. At the end of a hall, I debated whether to keep going or turn down a side corridor. An invisible leash yanked me forward, so I kept going straight. I passed my homeroom, the library, then made a left turn down a hall I'd never before noticed.

Darkness closed in, and I longed for one of my nightlights. My teeth were clenched tight to keep from chattering. At the end of the hall, I saw a tiny light. Was it a ghost or a reflection from one of the windows? Light bobbed back and forth, illuminating a figure holding a flashlight. Not a ghost, but a girl. Even with her long hair tucked underneath a cap, I recognized Danielle. Her light disappeared with her inside a room.

Follow her, I heard Opal order.

"Easy for you to say." I whispered to myself.

She needs help.

"I could use some help, too—and answers. Like what am I doing here?"

Hurry, was all Opal said before I felt her fade away.

I was too curious to turn around, so I slipped deeper into the hallway. Feeling along the wall, I stopped when I found a doorway. I saw a flicker of light and peered inside.

Danielle had entered a storage room. She aimed a small flashlight at a filing cabinet as she rifled through the top drawer. She seemed to know exactly what she was looking for. But I didn't have a clue, and Opal was totally AWOL. Why was Danielle sneaking around at night?

She moved to another drawer in the cabinet. In the faint light, I caught a glimpse of her face. Her eyes were determined. After a few minutes, she groaned with frustration and slammed this drawer shut. Then she yanked open another drawer and began searching all over again.

"Where?" I heard her say. "Where did he put it?"

She shoved the drawer and it shut with a metallic clank. I jumped, glancing over my shoulder nervously. I saw nothing except darkness in the hall, but my skin tingled and I had a creepy feeling.

When I glanced at Danielle again, she had moved on to another cabinet and was shuffling through more files. She pulled open the top drawer, then paused as if thinking hard. Or listening.

Then she whirled around and caught me in the glare of her flashlight

"Ohmygod!" she exclaimed. "Sabine?"

I blinked at the bright light. "Hey, you're blinding me!"

"How? Why?" Danielle sounded stunned. "What are you doing here?"

"I saw you come here and I was worried—worried you were in trouble."

"The only trouble I've got is you."

"Come on, let's get out of here," I whispered fiercely. Shielding my eyes, I added, "Shut off that flashlight so we don't get caught. Let's go—talk somewhere else." I couldn't think of what else to say.

"I've got nothing to say to you." She only lowered the light a few inches. "Go away."

"Not until you tell me why you're doing this."

"Butt out. This isn't any of your business. And don't you dare tell anyone you saw me here."

"I won't if you explain what's going on. Why did you break in here?"

"It's not breaking in when you have a key," she said defensively.

"If you have a key, why are you sneaking around?"

"I don't *want* to, but I have to. You wouldn't understand."

"Try me," I urged softly.

"I can't!" She shook her head. "I promised. Now leave before we both get into trouble."

"Too late," a gruff voice cut in. In the doorway loomed a hulking man wearing a gray uniform and holding a flashlight. The janitor—Mr. Watkins.

"You girls better talk fast and have a good explanation

before I call the cops," he said, stepping into the room and snapping on the overhead light.

"Uh…" I tried to think of something to say, but drew a blank.

"Please don't call the police," Danielle begged. "My parents would kill me."

"Ain't my problem." He shrugged. "Save it for the cops."

"No! Don't call them!" Danielle scooted closer to me, clutching my hand with sweaty fingers. "I wasn't doing anything wrong. Tell him, Sabine!"

I turned to her with bewilderment. "Tell him what?"

"About—the kid we saw sneaking around and how we chased him in here." Danielle was squeezing my hand so tight, I shook her off.

"A kid?" My heart thudded. "Oh, yeah. The kid."

"But he ran off before we could catch him," Danielle said quickly. "I think he was a vandal. He could have broken windows or started a fire, only we scared him away. Instead of giving us a hard time, you should be thanking us." She sounded so pathetic. Still, I nodded, playing along.

The janitor scowled. "You expect me to buy that load of crap?"

"That kid could still be around," Danielle warned, sticking to her ridiculous story. "Don't waste your time with us; go look for him before he gets away."

The janitor rubbed his beard and narrowed his gaze at us. "Enough. I'm calling the cops."

"But you can't!" Danielle sobbed.

"Watch me." He chuckled and reached for a cell phone in his pocket.

Danielle clutched at me. "Sabine, do something."

"I wish I could." Panic pounded with my heartbeats. If we were arrested, everyone would find out and ugly rumors would spread. Penny-Love might stick up for me, but some of the others would turn away. And Josh—what would he think? I'd die if he turned away, too. But there was nothing I could do.

Don't give up so easily, Opal told me. *Tell him that the police will find his car trunk interesting.*

"The police will find his car trunk interesting?" I questioned out loud, feeling like a total idiot but desperate enough to try anything.

The janitor stopped dialing and glared at me. "What did you say?"

"Nothing. Uh—just that if the police show up, they'll look everywhere." I thought fast. "Including your trunk."

"My car's got nothing to do with this," he growled.

"Pens, staplers, a phone, and a computer monitor," I repeated the message Opal passed on. Realization dawned, and I pointed my finger at the janitor. "You stole those things from the school?"

"Shut up!" He curled his hand into a fist. "You're a lying little bitch. One more word and I'll let you have it."

Danielle stared at me with wide eyes. "Sabine, stop saying scary stuff. You're making things worse."

"Listen to your girlfriend if you know what's good for you. Say one word about me to the cops, and I'll come after both of you."

He's bluffing, Opal told me. *Don't let him scare you. He has serious issues to overcome in this lifetime. He compensates for his inadequacies by thievery, going as far as stealing money from his mother's purse.*

"Stealing from his mother!" I exclaimed.

"Who told you that?" he demanded.

"You took money from your own mother's purse!"

"Why you little—" Mr. Watkins dropped his cell phone. He didn't move to pick it up, instead he raised his fist at me. "Get out!"

"But—But what about the police?" I stammered uselessly. "Aren't you going to call them?"

"Just go!" he shouted.

I grabbed Danielle, then we raced out of there. All I could think about was getting far away from that psycho janitor. I ran so fast, Danielle lagged behind.

"Hurry!" I heard the quickening of her footsteps.

Racing down the hall, around a corner, out of the school. Relief and gratitude filled me. Opal had truly been my guardian angel this time.

I didn't slow down until I reached the sidewalk. Only then did I stop, ready to get some answers from Danielle.

"After nearly getting me arrested, you owe me the truth," I said as I turned to face her. Only I was talking to air.

Danielle was gone.

9

When I reached home, the lights were off and my grandmother was already asleep. I found a Post-It note on my
door from Nona that said simply: "Mom called."

I'd spent the last hour breaking laws and risking arrest,
but none of that compared to the anxiety I felt at those two
words. I'd rather return to the school and face the psycho
janitor than call Mom.

My mother might have loved me, but she sure didn't
like me much. And who could blame her? I mean, I was the
weird one. My sisters were so much easier—sharing Mom's

love of music and performing. They even kept their rooms clean. But my room—and my life—had never been tidy. The imaginary friends of my childhood hadn't been imaginary, and I'd often known things—disturbing things, like our elderly neighbor falling down the stairs and lying there until I convinced my parents to check on her. Or the time I'd told my sisters' piano teacher that her daughter had a broken arm—minutes before the hospital called.

And I knew without being told that Mom was going to send me away. My bags were already packed when she gave me the news. Sure it hurt, but I didn't let her know. Never once did I argue. Instead it was Dad who took my side, accusing Mom of overreacting. But in the end, he preferred peace to war and quietly gave in to Mom's decision. Now my only contact from Mom was a monthly check to cover my expenses.

So why had she called now?

I awoke still wondering this the next morning. But I had no intention of picking up the phone to find out. If Mom had something important to say, she'd call back.

Deciding not to call Mom was easy; picking an outfit proved a bit difficult. After trying on four shirts, two skirts, and five pairs of pants, I finally settled on a scoop-neck yellow shirt and dark jeans. Then, I brushed on a bit of makeup. For a finishing touch, I fastened on tiny gold stud earrings. Tasteful—even attractive—but definitely not unusual.

When I caught a glimpse of myself in the mirror, I was

smiling—thinking of Josh and anxious to get to school. Would he be waiting by my locker?

He was. And his face lit up when he saw me.

Josh talked about his weekend as I sorted through my locker. He'd gone to a meeting of magicians and learned how to make empty shoes walk on air.

"Not really walk, of course, just appear to." He snapped his fingers. "Like magic."

"How can I tell if it's a trick or real magic?" I asked, grabbing my English book.

"Easy. There is no real magic."

I wondered if he'd say the same thing about psychics.

Josh went on to describe his great aunt's ninety-ninth birthday party. Instead of gifts, everyone came with a funny story or joke to share. His story involved a bowl of green Jell-O and a teacup poodle, and I was still laughing when we reached our first class. The teacher hadn't arrived, so we waited in the hall along with some other kids.

Josh tossed his backpack by the door, then turned back to me. "So how was your weekend?"

"Dull," I answered with a shrug. "No poodles or Jell-O."

"Nothing interesting?"

"Nope." Except for seeing a ghost and getting caught by the janitor for breaking into the school. I hesitated, then added, "Well, there was something funny."

"What?"

"My grandmother lost her notebook and I found it—in the refrigerator."

"Why'd she put it there?"

"So she wouldn't lose it." I giggled at his confused expression. "You had to be there, but believe me, it was weird even for my grandmother."

"I believe you." He squeezed my hand. And the way he was looking at me, we weren't talking about Nona anymore. My heart sped up as he leaned closer. We were standing in the middle of a school hallway, with kids all around, yet it was like we were alone. And I was sure he was going to kiss me.

"Sabine!" Penny-Love came rushing between us like a tornado, her curly red hair tangling around her freckled face. "Wait till you hear!"

"Hear what?" I said a bit sharply.

"Then you don't know? Wow! It's all over school!"

"I doubt that." Josh checked his watch. "School doesn't even start for ten minutes."

"The buzz doesn't run on school time." Penny-Love paused to catch her breath, then exclaimed, "Someone broke into the school last night!"

"Broke into …?" My legs almost buckled. "Oh, no!"

"Oh, yes. Dunlap is talking to the police right now."

"The police?" Dunlap was the principal. I felt sick. "They're here?"

"Two cops with guns and everything. Who do you think did it? Crime is only supposed to happen in big cities, not here. This is so exciting!"

Josh frowned. "What was damaged?"

"Windows were smashed, walls painted with swear-words, garbage cans knocked over, and they stole stuff from a supply room."

"But how could that happen when I was—" I clapped my hands over my mouth. "I mean—how could anyone do such a thing?"

"Shocking, huh?" Penny-Love shook her head, but the sparkle in her eyes was a dead giveaway she was enjoying this.

"Probably some punks from Regis High," Josh said with a scowl.

A few other kids had gathered around to listen, whispers spreading.

"This is more serious than a rival school prank," Penny-Love added ominously.

"Were there any witnesses?" Josh asked.

"Yeah. I heard a neighbor saw someone running out of the school. She thought it was a girl."

"She didn't get a good look?" I asked anxiously.

"Guess not." Penny-Love shrugged. "But there were paint handprints found by the supply room."

I glanced away, cursing myself for not washing my hands before leaving Jill's. Would the police be able to match the prints to mine? While I'd gotten in trouble at my previous school, I'd never been arrested. I didn't think my fingerprints were on file anywhere. Maybe I was safe... for a while. Besides, the worst I'd done was trespass, which technically wasn't breaking and entering since Danielle had a key. And nothing had been vandalized when we'd been there.

"What about the janitor?" I asked. "Why didn't he stop the vandals?"

"He didn't get a chance." Penny-Love lowered her voice. "Poor guy."

My pulse jumped. "What do you mean?"

"I guess the janitor must have caught them trashing the school." She paused before adding dramatically, "He was attacked and found unconscious. He'll be able to tell who did this when he wakes up. If he ever does."

10

A window in the computer lab had been smashed, and when I arrived for my sixth period newspaper/journalism class, a worker was hammering plywood over the window frame.

"Luckily the computers weren't damaged," Manny said, looking up from his keyboard. With barbed wire woven in his dreadlocks and carefully planned rips in his jeans, he had an edgy yet polished style that demanded attention. "Too bad about the vandalism and the janitor, but it makes a great story. I got out of my last class to work on it, and I'm almost finished."

"I hope you have the facts straight. The rumors have gotten so wild."

"Yeah. The popular guilt vote goes to the jocks from Regis High, but I don't think they'd attack the janitor."

I dumped my stuff at my desk, then came up beside Manny. "Did you interview the police?"

"Not yet. But Dunlap gave me enough info for my article. I can't believe how sloppy the vandals were. They left behind loads of evidence."

"They did?" I gulped. "Like what?"

"Read about it when you edit my piece." He hit a key and the printer started up. When it stopped, he handed me two full pages. "The sooner the better. Thanks in advance."

I nodded, already skimming the article with shaky hands. Manny had opened with basic information: location, time, date, and a description of the damage. He'd included a list of the missing items: from staplers to a television. Then it went on to describe the janitor's injuries: a bash on his head, cuts and bruises. He'd regained consciousness, but his memory was confused and the police hadn't been able to get any answers from him.

Chills crawled up and down my skin. Mr. Watkins might have stolen supplies, but he hadn't attacked himself. What if he were so confused he thought Danielle and I jumped him? I didn't even have an alibi. Nona had been asleep when I'd returned home. And I couldn't tell anyone why I'd left Jill's early. Who would believe a psychic vision led me to the school?

The words on the paper blurred as I fought to stay calm. I'd been in trouble before, accused of things I had no control over. "I won't let it happen again," I murmured, then flushed when I realized I'd spoken out loud.

"What did you say?" Manny swiveled in his chair to face me. "Did you find something wrong?"

"Not with your article."

But there was plenty wrong with my life, and I couldn't sit around waiting for the police to slap on the handcuffs. Last time I'd been accused unfairly, I'd stood by without defending myself. I'd counted on my parents to stand up for me, and I'd been disappointed. The only person I could count on was myself. I had to find out what really happened last night.

And I'd begin by questioning the person who'd gotten me into the mess.

*   *   *

Josh told me that Evan told him that Danielle was sick and wouldn't be at school for a few days.

"But here's her phone number," Josh added, walking to his car. When he wasn't busy after school, Josh liked to drop me off; then we'd talk on the phone later. I hadn't worked up the nerve to invite him in to meet Nona yet.

Fallen leaves crunched under my feet as I walked down my long gravel driveway. In the distant pasture, I saw Nona and Dominic tending to one of the cows. Good. No one would be around when I called Danielle.

I grabbed the phone and dialed the number Josh had given me.

"Crother residence," a man answered. Probably Danielle's father.

"Uh, hi. Is Danielle there?"

"Yes, but she isn't feeling well."

"Can I talk to her for just a minute? It's kind of important."

"Well … guess it can't hurt. I'll see if she's up to it. Hang on a minute."

It was more like four minutes before Danielle came on the line, coughing as she asked who was calling.

"Sabine," I told her. "We have to talk."

"Can't it wait?" Another cough. "I'm not feeling too hot. I have to go—"

"Don't hang up!"

"I think I'm going to vomit—"

"Stop the act. You're not really sick."

"Yes, I am!"

"Right," I said sarcastically. "And last night was only a bad dream. Don't put me off, Danielle. Or I'll just call back and talk to your father. I bet he'd be very interested to know his daughter broke into the school and—"

"No! You don't understand."

"That's for sure."

"You can't tell my parents anything. They think I was studying with a friend last night, and they'd be devastated if they knew I lied. They've got this unreal idea that I'm this perfect daughter, and I don't want to hurt them."

"I won't say anything—as long as you explain what happened. Things have gotten serious. Didn't you hear about the vandalism and the attack on the janitor?"

"Sure. Evan told me—but that doesn't involve us. We were already gone."

"Only we can't prove that. It doesn't sound like the janitor remembers much, but what if he tells the police we were there? We could get blamed for everything."

"But that's wrong!" she exclaimed shrilly. "We weren't even there when that stuff happened."

"If anyone finds out we were there at all, we could be in big trouble. Expelled or even arrested."

"Ohmygod! I—I'd die if it got that bad," she whispered. "Oh, Sabine... What can we do?"

"You can tell me what you were really looking for last night."

There was a long pause on the other end of the phone, and I had an image of Danielle huddled under a patchwork quilt, clutching a pillow to her chest with trembling hands. Her pale face was tear-stained and a dinner plate was untouched beside her bed.

"You win," she finally said in a weary tone.

Then she told me.

*　　　*　　　*

Danielle was a liar and a cheat.

Or at least she planned to cheat by stealing an important test from her bio teacher. By working in the school office, she'd learned that the only copy of the test was hidden in a locked storage room. So she'd "borrowed" a key from the office. Her plan seemed simple: go to the room after school, sneak inside, and copy the test. No one would know, and she'd ace her bio test.

Only, I'd come along and caught her in the act. She'd lied and manipulated me into helping her. I should have been angry, but she sounded so miserable that I just felt sad for her. Also, I felt relieved because this time I'd acted on my vision and maybe prevented Danielle from running into the vandals and being attacked like the janitor.

Danielle begged me to keep her secret, and because I had secrets of my own to protect, I agreed.

Still I wondered who vandalized the school. I turned this problem over in my mind as I lay on my bed staring up at the ceiling. My eyes ached and blurred. Shutting them, I went over last night's events. Over and over, trying to untangle questions, straighten them into answers—but only getting more questions. Where had Danielle gone after she left me? Did the janitor see who attacked him? Was it one person or a gang? I visualized a paint-splattered wall with ugly scrawled messages.

A banging door from downstairs snapped my concentration. Nona must have come in from the pasture to start dinner. She was a terrific cook and she'd promised to make my favorite tonight—lasagna. My mouth watered as I anticipated cheesy noodles, vegetables, and homemade sausage. Although we had a formal dining room table, we always ate on the big porch, watching the sunset. Dominic never joined us, which suited me fine.

Since moving here, my relationship with Nona had grown into a close friendship. She told me we had a strong connection that went back into past lives. We'd been sisters, mother and daughter, and even married. I'd laughed, pretending not to believe. But I had no doubt that our bond went deep and long ago.

All this would end if I had to leave.

I should offer to help with dinner, I thought. But if I go downstairs now, Nona's radar will pick up my anxiety in a heartbeat.

So I reached for my craft bag and channeled my nervous energy into embroidery. Needle in and needle out, twisting, twirling yarn into delicate designs. My mind wove patterns, too. Incriminating evidence was stacked against me. I'd been in the storage room and left behind paint marks. A witness might have seen me. And I'd argued with the janitor, who was now hospitalized.

"Not looking good," I murmured as I snipped a silver yarn with scissors.

Staring down at the white landscape, I saw shapes that weren't there at a first glance. An owl flying in a blizzard and a snow bunny nibbling on a lone blade of frosted grass. Things became clear when you looked beyond the obvious.

That's what I should do, too. Search deeper than the surface for answers. And I couldn't rely on Opal or confusing psychic visions. There was no controlling my gift, only learning to live with it—which I didn't want to do. The more I used my sixth sense, the stronger it would become. Then I'd never be free of other worlds.

"Sabine, can I come in?"

Glancing up, I saw Dominic standing in my doorway.

"What are you doing here?" I asked ungraciously.

He shifted his feet, looking uncomfortable. "I want to ask you something."

"Make it quick." I gestured to my embroidery. "I'm kind of busy here."

"It's about what you said—about seeing my mom."

"Forget it. I was hallucinating."

"That's what I thought…at first." He stepped closer and although he wasn't as tall as Josh, he filled my room with a strong presence. "But then I found something odd."

My needle slipped, lightly jabbing my finger. I winced. "What?"

"This." He handed me a silver coin. "It was in my pocket."

"So what? It's just an ordinary nickel."

"You *know* it's more. It's dated the year I was born."

"I have no idea what you're talking about." The coin tingled in my palm, and I tossed it back to him without looking at it.

He caught it and eyed me accusingly. "You know a lot of things, don't you?"

I pointed to the door. "Get out."

"I'm not going anywhere until you explain. How did you know about my mother? Did Nona tell you? Was it all some kind of trick? Or did you really see her?"

"You were there. Figure it out."

"I think I have," he said quietly. "But I can't figure out why you lied to your grandmother about losing your gift."

"I have no idea what you're talking about." I folded my arms across my chest. "And who'd believe you anyway?"

"No one has to believe *me.*" He glanced at my shelves with nightlights, brushing his callused fingertips over the spiked fin of a shark nightlight. "You're going to tell your grandmother."

"Am I?"

"Yes. And you have just twenty-four hours."

"Or what?" I demanded sarcastically. "You'll tell on me?"

"If I have to," he said with an expression as impossible to read as his falcon's.

"Go ahead. My grandmother will never believe you over me."

"You sure about that? Haven't you wondered why Nona invited me to live here?"

"No," I lied.

"Part of the reason is that she knew my mother. But the other part has to do with unusual gifts and Nona asked me not to tell you. She worried you'd be upset because you weren't psychic anymore." He snorted. "I guess the joke's on her."

I dug my fingers into my embroidered cloth. "What goes on between Nona and me isn't your business."

"It became my business when she asked me to take your place."

"My place?" His words were a hammer slamming into my heart.

"You're so busy running around with your friends, dating that lightweight who only plays at magic, you don't know what's going on with your own grandmother. You told her you lost your gift when she needed you. So she chose a different apprentice, someone she could trust with her secrets."

"You?" I whispered.

He nodded solemnly.

"But why?"

"That's for her to explain. I've already said too much." He reached for the doorknob. "If you haven't told Nona by tomorrow, I will."

Then he strode out of the room, leaving me with my mouth hanging open.

I glanced at my watch and felt sick inside. I couldn't face Nona, but I'd have to—in twenty-three hours and fifty-nine minutes.

11

Just another day at school. The halls were crowded with kids hanging out or rushing to classes, and Josh met me at my locker. I smiled as he launched into a funny story about his dog "Horse." Josh was so easy to be around and I loved his sense of humor—something that Dominic clearly did not have.

Thinking of Dominic knotted my stomach. Trouble was closing in fast—at school and home. At least at school, I could pretend everything was okay. No one had connected the paint handprints to me, the janitor remained in the hospital, and Danielle was still skipping school.

By the afternoon, my fake smile was ready to crack. I was tired of talking about everything except what was really on my mind. And I was no closer to solving the crime. I mean, what did I know about investigation? Nothing. I needed help, only there was no one to turn to. Penny-Love was a great friend, but she was an even greater gossip. Josh could be trusted—but would he still trust me if he knew what I'd been hiding? And the one person who had guessed my secret was the last person I'd confide in.

To my surprise, help came from an unexpected source.

Since I was in no hurry to go home, I told Josh I had extra work to do for the newspaper. I went into the computer lab and found the staff sports reporter, Yvette, sorting through photographs with Manny. Yvette was a tall, sharp-faced sophomore with a keen eye for detail and an ever-present camera strapped over her shoulder. She and Manny had a difference of opinion over the front-page photo, but after a heated discussion, they compromised by using two pictures. Then Yvette grabbed her stuff and left.

Manny shut down his computer, turned as if to leave, but stopped when he noticed me. "Sabine, what are you doing here?"

"Uh, work."

"What work?" He looked at my desk. "I didn't assign you anything new."

"I know, it's not really that—it's something else." My head ached. "I just needed to be alone."

"Tough day?" His tone softened as he pulled up a chair beside me. "Pour it all out to Mystic Manny."

"Mystic!" My laugh was bitter. "You have no idea. If you did, you'd never let anyone call you that again."

"Maybe I don't really know the future, but I'm not blind. And I can tell that you're upset. Is there trouble in Josh-Land?"

"No. He's great."

"So what's the problem?"

I sighed. "Me."

"Not possible." The barbed wire in his braids jingled as he shook his head firmly. "I don't believe that for a minute. You're the hardest worker on the paper, always ready to help, and the only one who doesn't ever complain. If I were the pope, I'd grant you sainthood."

"Or burn me as a witch," I murmured.

"What's that supposed to mean?"

"Nothing." I jumped up. "I better go."

"Not this time, Sabine." He gently eased me back in my chair. "You never explained about the dragonfly tattoo and why you freaked out last week. And don't think I haven't noticed other things."

My heart jumped. "What things?"

"How you never talk about your family or your last school. So I did a little checking—you understand, just building skills for my future as an investigative journalist—and I uncovered some interesting information."

I drummed my fingernails on the desktop, not meeting his gaze. Fighting the urge to cover my hands over my ears, I forced myself to act calm.

"Nice, quiet Sabine turns out to be—and I quote: 'Disruptive and dangerous to other students.' That was from the principal at your last school."

"You can't believe anything he said. He was a moron."

"You were also accused of being delusional and ordered to see a shrink."

"I only went once. She was a moron, too."

"A group of students petitioned to have you expelled."

"So what?" I shrugged. "I can't expect everyone to like me."

"Well, *I* like you." Manny chuckled. "Even more now that I know you have a dark side."

"Really?" I asked in a quiet voice, not really believing him. When friends found out you were different, they were afraid, they turned away.

But Manny wasn't going anywhere. "You're one twisted chick." His grin widened. "How did you manage to turn an entire school against you? I'd love to hear that story."

"You couldn't handle it."

"Beany, I can handle anything—and anyone."

I stared at him, a wild idea popping into my head. He really did have a talent for investigating. Sure, he was stuck on himself and strutted around with an ego ten times the

size of the football field. But underneath it all was resource-
fulness and friendship. He had the skills to help me find out
who vandalized the school before suspicion fell on me. And
looking for vandals would help keep my mind off my other
problems.

So I gave him exactly what he wanted.

The truth.

*   *   *

Instead of looking at me like I was crazy, Manny hugged me.
"You're a miracle! I've been wishing for you my whole life."

"I hope that's not a pick-up line, because it really sucks,"
I tried to joke. But my pulse was racing.

"That's not what I mean." His dark eyes shone as he
stared off toward a window. "The Mystic Manny column
is only the beginning. Then it's on to fame, fortune, and a
Pulitzer Prize. With your talent and my brains, anything is
possible."

"Hold it right there." I put out my hand. "What I told
you is confidential."

"But you said you wanted to work together."

"Yes, only it's a secret. No one finds out I'm—I'm different. I'll give you real predictions for your column if you help
me find out who vandalized the school."

"Don't you just know?" he asked.

"I only know what I'm allowed to know." I read the confusion on his face and tried to explain. "I can't tell when
I'm going to get a vision and then the images are confus-

ing. Like I saw a bloody dragonfly, and had no idea what it meant until I met Danielle and saw her tattoo. Then another vision led me to the school. I think I did what I was supposed to, but I'm never sure."

"Are visions the only way you get psychic messages?"

"No. Sometimes I'm contacted by ghosts or spirits."

"Aren't they the same thing?"

I shook my head. "Ghosts are confused—usually afraid to leave Earth to go on to the other side. Spirits are already on the other side, but they can come back to visit. Some are guides, like my spirit guide, Opal."

"Does she watch over you like an angel?"

"Oh, she's watching all right—but she's far from angelic. She has this major attitude and says I have to learn from my mistakes, yet she won't give me any hints about my own future. I know she loves me, I just wish she weren't so bossy and critical."

"Sounds like my dad." He laughed as he pulled a chair over to sit across from me. "I'm glad I don't have a spirit guide."

"Oh, you do." I closed my eyes and concentrated. I couldn't control my visions, but I could usually get a sense of spirit guides. "His name is William."

"Are you kidding me?"

"No, I'm serious. He has a dark beard and a mole on his nose. He used to be a farmer until he took a vow of celibacy and became a monk."

"Celibacy? You mean, none—not *ever?*"

"Yeah."

"Poor guy." Manny looked up into the air. "Willy, if you're listening, just know that I really feel for you."

I laughed. Manny may be shallow, but he was so honest about it, you couldn't help but like him.

"How do we start investigating?" I asked, clasping my hands in my lap.

"Talk to people, search online, examine the crime scene." He pulled out a small notebook and pen from his pocket. "Keep track of everything you learn in a notebook. Dig around for holes."

"Holes?"

"Yeah," he said seriously. "It's not so much the facts you're looking for, but the gaping questions that nag you."

"Like why did the school get vandalized after I left?"

"Exactly. Is that a coincidence or a clue?"

I shrugged. "Don't know."

"So we'll find out. I'll check out the crime scene and talk to that neighbor who witnessed someone running away—"

"Me." I sighed. "She saw me."

"You don't know that for sure. Anymore than you can be sure about Danielle. Sneaking into the supply room seems highly suspicious."

"I won't break my promise to Danielle, but she told me why she was there. It wasn't honest, just not a major crime. She didn't break windows or paint graffiti. And she definitely didn't attack the janitor."

"The janitor." Manny made a notation in his notebook. "I'll check him out, too."

"But he's the victim. You can't possibly suspect him?"

"Not really. But he chewed me out once for spitting, and I've never liked him."

"He is a jerk. And a thief, too, if what Opal told me is true. She said his car trunk was full of stolen school supplies—probably some of the stuff they think the vandals took."

"I'll look into that, too," Manny said. "And there's something you should do, even if you don't want to."

I eyed him cautiously. "What?"

"There isn't much point in having a gift if you don't unwrap it." He wagged his pencil at me. "Use your powers."

12

I thought about my talk with Manny as I walked home.

It was amazing how comfortable he was with psychic ability. Not freaked out or afraid I was going to read his mind. He acted like it was a thrilling game. Maybe to him, but not to me. It was hard enough to survive in this world, much less deal with other worlds, too. I'd use my "powers" for the Mystic Manny column as I promised, but that was all.

"I don't need your help, Opal," I thought. "You can sit on the sidelines and watch while I use my other five senses to find the vandals."

The smell of spicy herbs filled the house when I stepped inside. I found Nona in the kitchen, whistling while she stir-fried vegetables and rice in a skillet. I knew she was making a large batch so she'd have plenty left over for Dominic. She never talked about it, but I'd noticed her taking food out to the barn.

Dominic.

He'd given me until six o'clock—or else. And the clock on the VCR showed 5:49.

I could hope he was bluffing. But that was a slim hope. Dominic took himself too seriously for idle threats. I could almost respect him for being protective of my grandmother, if he hadn't acted so high and mighty about it. But if anyone was going to talk to Nona, it was going to be me.

"Need a hand?" I asked my grandmother as I entered the kitchen.

Nona turned from the stove with a smile. "Thanks, but I have it under control."

"Smells yummy."

"It's almost ready. Then later, I have tons of work to do for a new client who is so demanding it's driving me crazy. He doesn't want a wife who's too tall or too thin or paints her toenails. He insists that she be college-educated, but not too brainy. And she has to have a June birthday. Tough nut to crack, but I think I found his match. As long as I can convince her to stop painting her toenails."

"Do you hear wedding bells yet?" I asked. Nona could always tell when her matchmaking efforts were on track because tinkling bells would ring in her head. If it was a soul-mate match, she'd also get a vision of white doves.

"Not even a jingle." She put the lid on the pot. "Maybe by tomorrow."

"I have lots of confidence in you. It's amazing how you bring people together. And your clients are always so grateful, inviting you to their weddings and that one lady named her daughter after you. I really admire how hard you work and—"

"Sabine, what are you trying so hard not to tell me?" She wiped her hands on a dishcloth, and fixed me with a deep look. "Something is troubling you."

"Stop reading me."

"Is everything okay at school?"

"Great."

"And with your new beau?"

"Even greater."

"So why is your aura out of alignment? I get a definite sense of conflict. What are you afraid of?"

I crossed to the table and sank wearily in a chair. The clock on the microwave showed 5:52. "Nona, you're right. I am afraid—of telling you something."

"Never be afraid to tell me something."

"But you're going to hate me."

"Rubbish. I could never hate you. No matter what you've done, I'm here for you." She put her hands on my shoulders. "What is it, honey?"

"I lied." I sucked in a deep breath, then blurted out the

rest before I lost my nerve. "When I was little and told you I saw ghosts and had an invisible friend, you were the only one who believed me. You made me feel like it was normal to talk to my spirit guide. But everyone else freaked out—especially Mom. Then I got into trouble at school, scaring people by knowing stuff. And that boy died."

"It wasn't your fault."

I glanced away, swallowing hard.

"Besides that's all in the past," Nona added, giving my shoulders a reassuring squeeze. "You don't have to deal with it anymore."

"Yes, I do." My voice trembled. "Nona, I still talk to Opal and know things before they happen. I hate myself for deceiving you, but I never lost my gift. Can you forgive me?"

Her hazel eyes narrowed thoughtfully. There was a ding from the timer and she turned to check on the simmering sauce. Then she fixed her gaze back on me and said, "There's nothing to forgive."

"Go ahead and yell at me. I deserve it."

"You don't owe me an apology."

"I owe you much more! You were so disappointed when I said I lost my powers and couldn't carry on the family gift. And you brought Dominic here as some sort of an apprentice. Only you don't need him anymore because you have me."

"I was afraid of this," Nona said with a sad shake of her head. "You found out I was mentoring Dominic and you're jealous."

"No! That's not it at all."

"You don't resent his being here?"

"Well…a little." I paused. "But that's not the issue. In fact, Dominic was the one who insisted I tell you the truth."

"Honey, you don't have to pretend for me. I love you even if you didn't inherit my gift."

"But I did!" I argued. "I was lying before, not now."

She gently squeezed my hand. "Sabine, you're my grand-daughter and I adore you more than the universe. I'll admit, I was disappointed when I found out you'd lost your psychic ability, but I've accepted it. And you have to, too."

"But I didn't *lose* anything. I still see ghosts. I talk to Opal all the time. I get strange visions."

"Are you sure? Or do you only want to think you have your gift?"

"I don't think anything—I know. Why can't you believe me?"

"I want to, honey, but I'll need more." She put her hands on her hips and gave me a challenging look. "Prove it."

13

If Opal weren't already dead, I would have killed her.

She could have said something—anything at all!—to convince my grandmother that I was in contact with the other side. Instead, she slammed an "Out to Lunch" sign on our communication channel. I begged and pleaded with her, yet nothing worked.

So I tried to summon a spirit.

I visualized a protective white light shielding me like armor against any dark spirits. Most spirits were cool and eager to find someone who could understand them, maybe pass on a message to a loved one. But you never knew when a stinker would butt in.

Nona stood by with a patient, sympathetic expression while I concentrated hard. "Is anyone there?" I mentally called out.

Nothing.

"Can you hear me? I just want to talk."

But apparently no one wanted to talk with me. And I blamed Opal.

"You're doing this to get back at me for telling you to go away," I silently accused. "Go ahead. Play your games. I can do this on my own."

Nona gave me a pitiful glance, and that fueled my determination to prove myself. I snapped my fingers and gestured to the phone. "Watch this. I'll predict who's calling. Ask anyone to call but don't tell me who, and I'll guess who it is before the phone is answered."

"Aren't you taking this a bit too far?" she asked, amused.

"Not until you believe me."

"It's not that important. You're beautiful, healthy, and smart. You're wonderful without any extra powers."

"Call someone." I pointed to the phone.

She sighed, but did as I asked. She went into another room to call someone, careful to shut the door so I wouldn't overhear. And when the phone finally rang a few minutes later, I played the "Who's Calling" game I'd enjoyed since I was a child.

"It's a woman." I forced an image into my head. "She's blonde—in her thirties and she is...looking for romance."

I grabbed the receiver on the third ring—and nearly died when I recognized the voice on the other end. Gerby Weatherby was a balding, eighty-something, poker-playing pal of Nona's.

"The only romance he's ever after is the cozy union of a pair of aces," Nona said with a laugh as she thanked Gerby and hung up.

"But I was so sure..." My shoulders sagged. "How could I be wrong?"

"It's okay, honey." Nona hugged me, her hands warm from being near the stove.

"No. It's not." I looked around the room, seeing, hearing, feeling nothing.

Despite the comfort of Nona's arms, I'd never felt so alone.

*   *   *

How many times had I wished to be normal? No voices, ghosts, angels, or bossy spirit guides. Be careful what you wish for.

When the phone rang later, I didn't even try to guess who was calling. But I probably could have.

"You sound down," Josh said sympathetically.

"Just tired." I curled up with the phone on the living room couch.

"So go to bed early and dream of me."

"Always." I smiled.

We didn't really talk about anything in particular. Mostly, I enjoyed hearing his voice. He could read the phone book and make it sound interesting. We ended with plans to go out to the hospital on Saturday morning so I could watch Josh do magic for the kids.

When I hung up, I felt even more alone. I missed Josh already, but it went deeper than that. The down mood lingered throughout dinner. I didn't say much while Nona told me her good news about matchmaking Mr. Picky with a smart, easy-going Gemini woman. I half listened, toying with my food. There was an ache inside, as if I'd lost my best friend. And I caught myself several times tuning Nona out and straining to hear beyond ordinary sounds—hoping for a familiar bossy voice.

Before I went to bed that night, I tried to cheer myself by plugging in the goofy green frog nightlight Dad had found for me in Mexico. It had a crooked froggy grin and buggy, crossed eyes fixed on a fly perched on its nose. In a cozy glow of green, I climbed underneath cool covers and fell asleep to sweet thoughts of Josh.

Only my dreams took a dark turn and fluttered into a swarm of dragonflies—giant evil-eyed creatures. Blood and wings and danger. A monstrous dragon had Danielle in its claws, flying high beyond sky and stars. Then the claws opened and Danielle fell. She screamed, over and over, and I tried to catch her. But my arms wouldn't move, bound together, helpless.

I awoke to find the twisted covers binding my arms like ropes.

Struggling to untangle myself, I pushed the covers on the floor and waited for my heart to slow. I glanced around my room, then looked again because something had changed. My nightlight! I realized with a jolt. The cross-eyed frog had been replaced with an angel-winged nightlight.

"How did that—Opal! You did this!"

Closing my eyes, I looked for my spirit guide. I never actually saw all of her—just fuzzy bits and pieces; it was a sense of her presence that I wanted. Like a bat flying blindly at night by internal sonar.

"Opal, did you switch my nightlight?"

I never did like frogs, her voice came through strong and sassy. *Slimy creatures, caused plagues back in my day.*

"You're here!" I rejoiced. "I couldn't feel you. I thought you were gone."

I never left.

"Why didn't you answer?"

There wasn't anything of importance to say.

"That never stopped you before. And now Nona doesn't believe me."

It's not my place to interfere.

"You've been interfering my whole life. Why stop now?"

You have an odd way of showing gratitude. Let me remind you that I am here as your guide, not as your servant.

"What about being my friend? I needed you earlier and

you let me down. I started to doubt myself—thought maybe I *had* lost my gift, lost you."

You've lost nothing; in fact, you will gain a new gift soon—if you are wise enough to recognize good fortune.

"Nothing's been good lately. Thanks to you, Nona thinks I'm delusional, and my attempt at helping someone could end up getting me in big trouble."

True blessings appear in many forms and wisdom is in the journey. My dear child, you vex me to no end. You have much to learn.

A sigh and then she was gone.

Walking over to my wall, I plugged the green frog night-light back into the socket. Then I took the angel nightlight to bed with me, hugging it against my chest.

My best friend hadn't deserted me.

Opal was back.

14

During my first period class the next morning, I was called to the principal's office.

When the teacher gave me the message, I stood on shaky legs and looked over at Penny-Love. She whispered, "What's he want with you?"

"Haven't a clue," I lied.

"Weird. But it's probably nothing."

"Yeah." I hid my worry with a shrug. "Probably nothing."

"Dunlap is okay," she added as I shoved my book into my backpack. "Those rumors about him slamming a kid against a wall are exaggerated. And I don't think he really broke Nick's arm."

Gulping, I glanced over at Josh. He gave me a thumbs-up gesture.

As my footsteps echoed in the near-empty school hall, I had a déjà vu moment. Walking down a hall in a different school, passing students who pointed and stared. Fearful whispers. "Witch." "Voodoo Queen." "Devil's Daughter." "Freak." Summoned before a different principal, the school board, and a committee of "concerned parents." Reading a petition, but unable to finish because my eyes filled with tears. My mother arriving with clicking heels, then leaving with a slammed door. Her fury and shame directed at me as we drove away, never to return.

"The principal wants to see me?" I asked the secretary who glanced up from her computer when I entered the office.

"Are you Sabine Rose?"

"Yes."

With a black pen, she crossed off my name from a typed list. "Please go inside. He's expecting you."

I reached for the door and turned the knob.

"Good morning, Miss Rose," Principal Dunlap greeted in a hearty tone. He was not a typical high–school principal. He was nicknamed "the Cowboy" because he wore denim and cowboy boots instead of a suit and tie. A gold belt buckle gleamed with the outline of a bucking bronco as he stood and introduced a stocky uniformed man sitting off to the side. "Let me introduce Officer Peters. He'd like to ask you a few questions."

"About what?" I asked, afraid I already knew the answer.

"Sunday night's vandalism and the assault on Mr. Watkins."

Oh, that, I thought nervously.

"Nothing to be nervous about," the principal added. "Only some routine questions. Are you comfortable with that?"

"I—I guess."

Officer Peters gestured for me to sit across from him and picked up a pen and notepad. "Where were you Sunday evening around nine-thirty?"

"At a friend's house. But what does this have to do with—"

"Jillian Grossmer," he interrupted in a crisp tone. "1396 Sapphire Way. Attending a cheerleading meeting?"

"Yes."

Dunlap drummed his fingers on his desk. "But you aren't a cheerleader."

"They're my friends. So I hang out with them." I clasped my hands, staring down at my fingers, remembering paint smudges.

"Miss Grossmer confirmed that," Officer Peters said, reading from his notes. "She also said that you left early."

"Yes."

"Did you walk home?"

"Yes. It's not too far."

"You reside with your grandmother." Another glance at his notes. "At 29 Lilac Road?"

"Uh-huh." My heart quickened, and I wished I could

read his mind. But I was too nervous to know my own thoughts, much less understandsomeone else's.

Officer Peters stood swiftly and reached around back—and I sucked in a deep breath, expecting him to grab handcuffs and read me my rights. But all he held out was a photograph. "On your walk home Sunday, did you happen to see any of these individuals?"

It was a photo of a group of jocks from our rival school. Relieved, I answered truthfully, "No."

"Are you acquainted with any of these young men?"

I shook my head.

"But you know who they are?"

"Who doesn't? Our football team slaughtered their team thirty-two to seven."

"On your walk home last night, did you notice anyone suspicious entering or leaving the school?"

"No. No one at all."

And then I was excused.

*　　*　　*

At lunch, everyone was still talking about the vandalism. It turned out that a lot of students had been questioned, so it wasn't just me. I wasn't even a suspect. Yet.

During my journalism class, I pulled Manny aside and asked anxiously, "Have you found out anything?"

"I'm working on it. I got some ideas who might be involved."

"Who?"

"Can't talk here." He looked around. "Meet me by the library after school for a surprise."

"New information?"

"Even better." He smiled wickedly. "Get ready to be blown away."

An image of ruby red flower petals with long thorny stems popped into my head, and I smelled roses. "What do roses have to do with it?"

He wagged a finger at me. "No using your woo-woo powers on me."

"I wasn't! Images just pop in my head sometimes."

"Try to imagine some fame and fortune in my future," he teased. Then someone called his name and he left.

During class, I thought about the roses. Was it a clue? Had the vandals hidden something in a rose bush? Did they live near a rose garden? Or did it have something to do with my last name, "Rose"? But that didn't feel right. The connection wasn't to me.

When the final bell rang, I hurried to my locker, dumped the books I didn't need for homework, and went straight to the library.

When I saw Manny, I almost turned around because he wasn't alone. He was deep in conversation with a Goth girl I'd seen a few times around school. Her dramatic appearance screamed "I'm a freak and proud of it!" Her sleek black hair glittered with gold sparkles and her eyes were shaded in heavy black kohl shadows. Gaudy rings crowded on her petite fingers, gold hoops pierced through her eyebrows, and a metal chain dog collar encircled her neck.

I ducked behind a corner, curious. Was Manny part of the Goth crowd? I didn't think so. From what I knew of him, he purposely shunned all groups, creating his own unique style. So maybe this girl had some information about the vandalism.

"Hey, Manny," I said, stepping forward.

"There you are." Manny waved. "We've been waiting."

"So you're Sabine." The girl studied me, her gray eyes narrowed critically. "Manny was telling me about you."

"Oh?" I shot Manny a warning look.

"Yeah. Like how you help him on the *Shout-Out.*" She looked at me hard for a few moments, as if sizing me up. "Is that your natural hair color?"

I nodded. Manny was just looking at both of us, a slight smile on his face.

"That black streak is wicked," she added. "With some streaks of red—"

"Thanks, I like my hair the way it is," I said, sounding unintentionally bitchy.

"Suit yourself." She rolled her eyes as she turned to Manny. "Listen, Manny, I gotta go."

"Not yet." Manny grabbed her arm.

"I should be the one to go," I said uncomfortably.

"Neither of you is going anywhere. Not until I tell you my surprise," he insisted "Or actually introduce her."

"Her? Your surprise is a person?"

"Yeah." Manny gestured with a dramatic sweep of his arm to the Goth girl. "Sabine, meet Thorn. Your new partner."

15

"I don't need a partner—or want one." Especially her, I almost added.

"I'll grow gray hair if I hang around her." Thorn said, looking at me with an arch in her pierced eyebrows. "Manny, I told you it wouldn't work out."

"Give this a chance, guys." Manny told us firmly. "You have a lot more in common than you realize."

"No way!" Thorn and I said at the same time. Startled, we stared at each other before looking quickly away.

"See? Almost like twins and you only just met." Manny

laughed. "Now shut up for a minute and let's get down to business."

"What business?" I asked cautiously.

"Investigating the vandalism. But not the usual way." He glanced around as some kids walked by, then lowered his voice. "Using your talents."

I glared at him. "You promised not to tell!"

"I didn't. But I know you'll want to when you see what Thorn can do. She has an amazing ability. It'll blow you away."

"I seriously doubt that."

Thorn curled her purple lips into a smug smirk, like she knew more than I did. "It'll be fun watching you choke on your own words."

"Not as fun as watching you fail." I lifted my chin in challenge. "Go ahead—try to amaze me."

"It'll be easy." She grinned. "What I do is called psychometry. That means I can find—"

"I know what it means," I cut in. "The ability to sense things by touch."

"Not bad. Most people have never heard of it." Thorn gave me a cautious, appraising look. "Anyway, I've been able to sense things by touch since I was little. I used to do it for kicks or to mess with people. It's a great party trick, too."

"Sure. Whatever." I shrugged, not buying this for a minute. If Thorn were psychic, I'd eat my backpack.

Thorn shook her head. "Just for the record, I'm only doing this for Manny because he's a real friend." She added coldly, "You have five minutes to hide an object."

"Like what?"

"A book, pen, a shoe—doesn't matter. Don't tell me what is it or where you plan to hide it."

"Okay." I nodded.

"Your five minutes start now." She glanced at one of her rings that doubled as a tiny clock. "When you're done, come back here."

She gestured for me to go, so I took off down the hall. I kept turning corners, hoping to confuse her if she was following. This whole game was dumb and I would rather walk out of the school gate and keep going till I reached home.

I went outside into a grassy quad area and rummaged through my backpack. At the very bottom, there was an oddly shaped piece of scuffed aluminum. It was an old epée grip. The epée had been my favorite weapon in fencing class at my old school, and this grip had been my teacher's. He'd given it to me. Mr. Landreth was the only person at that school who hadn't turned on me when things got bad. He'd believed in me and my gift. I don't know why I kept the grip in my pack—I just never really wanted to take it out and put it with all the other fencing stuff I never used anymore.

Thorn would never be able to find it. I looked around for a hiding place

Crouching down to hide the grip under a bench, I got a better idea. Minutes later, I returned to the library entrance where Manny and Thorn waited on a bench. When they saw me, they stood and hurried over.

"Well?" Manny prompted. "Mission accomplished?"

"Yes—it's hidden." I couldn't help but grin. Thorn

would never find it. I couldn't figure out how she'd conned a smart guy like Manny. But she couldn't fool me.

"Let me touch your hand that held the missing object," Thorn said. When I hesitated she added, "Don't worry, I won't *contaminate* you."

"You don't worry me."

"Are you sure?"

I ignored her laugh and boldly held out my right hand.

She traced the lines on my palm with her fingers, her black hair falling forward and brushing across my arm. "You hid something small. It had a funny shape."

"Well, that narrows it down."

"It's very important to you."

Startled, I tried to keep my expression calm. "Yeah."

Manny was grinning. "See, I told you she was cool."

"Come on, that's an easy guess." She couldn't be for real. I tried to rally my skepticism. "Besides what does she mean 'important to you'? Sounds like Mystic Manny—pure fortune cookie."

"Whatever, Sabine. Thorn knows."

"Then she should be able to find it." No way, I thought with secret delight. Thorn could search the whole school and she'd never figure out my hiding place.

After staring down the hall, Thorn turned to me with a shake of her dark head. "I have the strangest urge to look in a bathroom sink. Something is in the sink."

"Sink?" I laughed. "You are so far off."

"Not your thing. Something else missing…" Her voice

trailed off and she rubbed the center of her forehead. "Okay, I'm getting a sense of it. It's metal. It's old, well used, and it's somewhere dark and warm."

I didn't say anything. I nonchalantly moved my hands behind my back.

"How about the science lab?" Manny guessed.

"No," Thorn said. "Not a classroom. Not the cafeteria."

Pursing my lips tight, I gave nothing away.

She studied me. "You went outside, but that's not where you left it."

I just shrugged.

"It's close by," Thorn said, pacing around me. "Very close."

"But she couldn't hide whatever it is around here without us seeing her," Manny pointed out.

"Unless she hid it before she returned." Thorn's gaze zeroed in on my backpack, which I'd dumped on the floor. She walked to it, then paused and suddenly whirled around.

Thorn came directly towards me. Before I could say anything, she reached inside the pocket of my hooded sweatshirt and withdrew the grip. Any effort to look unimpressed was useless now.

"All right!" Manny pumped his fist.

"Did you ever doubt me?" asked Thorn.

"Not for a second," said Manny. "Now what the heck is that?"

I ignored Manny's question. "How did—did you ... ?" My words trailed off.

"It's just a weird talent. Like some people can paint or

play the piano. I can find things." Thorn handed the grip back to me. "And you must have some weird trick, too, or else Manny wouldn't want us to be partners."

"Partners," I echoed with wonder. Maybe, just maybe, Manny wasn't totally demented.

I really looked at Thorn this time. Past the Morticia makeup, multiple piercings, and heavy chains—into her gray eyes. Amazingly honest eyes. And I knew with sudden clarity that I'd been completely wrong about her. She wasn't a fake.

I was.

And I remembered what Opal had said about my "gaining a new gift soon." I'd thought she meant some*thing*, not some*one*. Thorn?

Took you long enough, Opal said. *Your intuitive skills are getting rusty, certainly from lack of use. But there's hope for you.*

And when I told Thorn that I was psychic, she didn't call me crazy.

She believed.

*   *   *

When I got home later, Nona was frantically tearing up the house, looking for her missing car keys. She was positive she'd left them in her purse, only they weren't there. They weren't in any of her other usual hiding places, either. Not the cubby hole in the recliner, the toe of her slippers, or the fridge.

Something Thorn said jumped into my head.

I went straight to the bathroom sink.

And found the missing keys.

16

Ten minutes later, Nona was ready for a dinner date with a new client, and she thanked me again for finding her keys.

"Glad to help," I said from the couch where I was twisting my hair into a braid.

"If you get hungry, there's leftover rice in the fridge."

"Thanks, but I won't need it. Josh is taking me out."

"Oh, yeah. You have a date. I remember now." She glanced down at her keys, then gave a sheepish smile. "Guess I have too much on my mind. You and Josh have fun, but it's a school night so don't stay out too late."

"We won't," I promised, giving her a hug.

Then she rushed out to her car, and a short while later Josh showed up.

When we'd talked at school about going out, Josh acted all mysterious and wouldn't tell me what he had planned. He just said to wear outdoor clothes. So the first thing I asked as I fastened the seatbelt in his car was, "Where are we going?"

"Curious?" he asked teasingly, gravel crunching under his tires as he drove down our driveway.

"A little."

"Only a little?"

"Well…more than a little. Just tell me already. Are we going to play tennis, volleyball, or mini-golf?"

"Nope." He laughed, and I loved how dimples formed at the corners of his mouth. "Ever toss a Frisbee?"

"Of course."

"Good."

"So that's the big mystery?" I asked, a bit disappointed. "Playing Frisbee?"

"It's who you play with that matters."

"Why do I get the feeling you're not telling me something?"

"Guess you're psychic," he said with a laugh.

My face went hot and I glanced quickly out the window. He didn't seem to notice I wasn't laughing with him and reached across the seat for my hand. I held on tight, reminding myself this was what I wanted—to be a normal girl out with a cute, popular guy. It didn't matter that Josh didn't know all my secrets; in fact, I preferred it that way.

"If it's okay with you," he went on, "we'll grab some deli sandwiches and take them to a park."

"Sure!" I said a bit too brightly. "But isn't it kind of late in the day for a picnic?"

"We've got almost two hours of daylight."

"Okay. A picnic sounds great." I eyed him suspiciously, sure there was more to this than playing Frisbee in the park. But I'd find out soon enough.

Josh popped in a CD and turned up the music. After a quick stop at a deli, instead of heading toward the park by the high school, Josh turned into an upscale subdivision.

"Isn't this your neighborhood?" I asked with a puzzled expression.

"Yeah. I have to pick up a surprise at my house. You're gonna love him."

"Him?" I asked uncertainly, hoping this wasn't going to be another double date. "Someone else is going with us?"

"Not exactly someone." He grinned. "Horse."

"Oh—your dog!"

"Yeah." He smiled. "It's about time you two got to know each other."

"Cool surprise. I love dogs."

"Since he's triple the size of most dogs, there's more to love." Josh stepped out of the car, then turned back to me. "Wait here. I'll only be a sec."

I watched him go around the side yard and disappear

through a gate. I heard exciting barking and smiled to myself, guessing that Josh was being greeted by sloppy doggy kisses. When the gate opened minutes later, Josh was struggling to hold a leash attached to a huge dog that looked like a cross between a golden retriever and an elephant. Josh had only moved a few feet forward when someone called out his name.

Turning sideways in my seat, I spotted Evan Marshall coming over from the house next door. I leaned closer to my open window.

"Hey, Evan," Josh said, jerking hard on the leash and nearly falling over except Evan lunged forward to steady him. "Thanks."

"No prob." Evan slapped him on the shoulder. "So, where've you been lately? Haven't seen you around much."

"Busy, I guess." Josh shrugged. "How come you aren't at practice?"

"Cancelled, because Coach has a dentist appointment. But things are going great." Evan's face lit up. "Get this, some college scout is gonna show up at our next game. So we're totally working our butts off. Getting noticed so early in my career would be huge."

"Man, that's great! Good luck."

"Thanks. So where you and Horse headed?"

"The park."

"Cool. I don't have anything else to do, so I'll come along. Did you bring Horse's favorite Frisbee? I'm always blown away when he jumps like ten feet and catches it. He's the greatest dog."

"Yeah, he is—but the thing is … " Josh shifted uncomfortably and glanced at the car.

Evan followed his gaze and abruptly stopped smiling. "Oh. I see," was all he said. But his shoulders slumped like he'd just lost an important game, and I almost felt sorry for him.

"You can still—" Josh started to say.

"No." Evan frowned and shook his head. "You don't need me around."

"But we want you. We can make room in the car."

"Don't bother. I got stuff to do anyway." Then before Josh could protest, Evan turned and strode back to his house.

"Sorry about that," I told Josh after Horse was settled into the backseat.

"Nothing to be sorry about."

"I didn't mean to cause problems for you with Evan."

"It wasn't your fault," Josh said casually, but the furrow in his brow showed he was concerned.

"Evan thinks it is."

"He runs hot and cold. He'll get over it."

"I don't think he approves of me."

"How could he not? You're perfect."

I laughed wryly. "I'm far from perfect. You have no idea."

"The proper way to accept a compliment is to say 'thank you.'"

"Thank you," I said with a smile.

"See," Josh said after Horse gave a sharp bark from the back seat. "Even Horse agrees with me, so don't worry about Evan. He'll be fine."

Still, I was worried—not because I cared if Evan liked me. To be honest, I didn't like him much and would be happy never seeing him again. But I cared about Josh and knew his friendship with Evan meant a lot to him. Growing up together and dealing with the loss of Josh's brother had created a deep bond. If Evan continued to resent me, it could cause serious problems.

And I wondered . . .

If it came down to a choice between Evan and me—who would Josh choose?

17

The next morning, I found out that Josh wasn't the only one with friendship issues. When I headed for school, Penny-Love was waiting for me by Nona's mailbox. I could tell by the way she stood with her hands on her hips and her lips puckered into a pout that something was up.

"I have a confession to make," she said bluntly.

"About what?"

"How I've been feeling—not that you've noticed," she accused. "Since you hooked up with Josh, you've forgotten about me. We're supposed to be best friends."

"We are—the very best."

"Then how come you're suddenly so busy? I had to get up early just to meet you this morning and you haven't been over to my house in a week. If you aren't with Josh, you're talking on the phone with him."

"Well, we *are* going out. Josh isn't spending much time with his friends, either."

"It's not just Josh. You're always busy with newspaper work, too."

"I went to your cheer club meeting," I reminded her.

"Which you ran out on early without telling me why."

"Sorry." I squeezed her hand. "I didn't know you were feeling this way."

"Now you know, so don't shut me out anymore. And there's another thing." She moved aside so a trio of elementary kids could pass. Once the kids were out of range, she said in a hushed tone, "I have to ask you something, even though it's gonna sound crazy."

"Crazy?" My heart jumped with the worry that she'd found out my secret. At my last school I'd had this friend, Brianne, and people thought we were sisters because we were together so much—until she found out about me. I don't know if she was scared of me or bitter because I'd kept something from her. When I saw the petition to get me kicked out of school, her name was on the first page.

"You're gonna laugh when I tell you," Penny-Love said. "I mean, one of the things I admire about you is your easygoing attitude. I have my drama moments, but never you. You're the most normal person I know, so I'm sure the rumor is totally untrue."

"Rumor?" I managed to smile like I was amused. "What?"

"A friend of Jill's saw you hanging out yesterday with a Goth freak. I told Jill her friend was mistaken, that it must have been someone else because you wouldn't be caught dead with one of those losers."

"Well . . . " I hesitated. "Thorn isn't a loser."

"Are you *serious?* You're too busy for me, but you find time to hang out with someone named *Thorn?*"

"I barely know her. She's helping with a—a project."

"What project?"

"With the newspaper. It was Manny's idea."

"So this is Manny's doing. Is she his latest girlfriend?"

"No, just a friend."

"As long as she doesn't become your friend, too." Penny-Love picked up her backpack, and we started walking. "For a second there you had me worried. Afraid you'd gone over to the dark side."

"Never happen." I glanced away guiltily. Maybe I should have said something more to defend Thorn, but I didn't want to hurt Penny-Love, and she was already sensitive about our friendship. So I smoothed things over by inviting her to my house tonight.

"Great! I've been curious about that guy your grandmother hired. If he's the hottie I spotted out in the pasture on my way here, I've got to meet him."

"Bad idea. Dominic is rude and totally antisocial."

"Oh, a challenge!" She rubbed her hands together. "Nothing I like better—especially when he's fine."

"You'll just be asking to be shot down. He's not your type."

She didn't argue, but the gleam in her eyes worried me.

*　　*　　*

The rest of the school day made me feel like a circus juggler, only instead of balls, I juggled people. Passing notes to Penny-Love in homeroom, admiring Josh's latest magic trick, and listening to my teachers so I didn't miss any assignments. Wearing a permanent smile, always hiding a part of myself. This was especially hard with Josh because when he looked at me, so sweet and caring, I'd long to tell him everything. Only I didn't dare.

At least there were no secrets with Manny, who still teased that I was his "miracle." After glancing around the classroom to make sure no one was watching, he handed me a paper from my "To Be Edited" folder, and I pretended to work while he clued me in on the latest news. "I accidentally found a memo to the principal from the police."

"'Accidentally'?" I couldn't help but grin. "Where? In his pocket?"

"On his desk."

"How did you manage that without getting caught?"

He smirked. "A journalist can't divulge professional secrets."

"So what did you learn?" I picked up a red pen and marked a misspelled word on the article.

"Regis High football players are cleared—partying that night with lots of witnesses. The janitor is out of the hospital, but has no memory of the attack. The police checked local pawnshops for the missing stuff—without success. They also received an anonymous tip saying that the stolen things were still at school."

"An anonymous tip?" I said, shivering despite the sun shining through the classroom windows. "I wonder who called it in."

"I was hoping you could tell me."

I shook my head. "It's not that easy."

"Well, if something comes to you, let me know. Recovering the missing items would make a great article." Manny leaned closer to whisper, "Which is why we're going to search the school tonight."

"*We* are?"

"Yeah—before anyone else does. Thorn's cool with the plan, and we're gonna meet in the Taco Bell parking lot at ten. Are you in?"

"Sure. As long as I don't have to do anything illegal."

"Misdemeanors only. And no one will find out."

"You're sure?"

"Trust me."

Not exactly encouraging words. But taking action was better than waiting around. So I nodded, and hoped I wasn't heading for trouble.

*   *   *

What was my grandmother doing on the porch with a paintbrush and a cow?

As I neared the house, I rubbed my eyes to make sure I wasn't hallucinating. Nona's gray-blond hair was wrapped in a bandanna and her oversized gray T-shirt brushed inches above the porch floor as she squatted on a low stool to paint blue, pink, and yellow flowers on her cow, Daphne.

I had to ask, even though I wasn't sure I wanted to know the answer. "Nona, what's going on?"

"I'm painting."

"On a cow? Can't you use a canvas like normal people?"

"Most people aren't as sensitive to the needs of their pets as I am." Nona patted Daphne's tawny head. "Poor dear was feeling like a plain Jane next to Stormy so I'm giving her a make over."

"But Stormy is a horse."

"*Shhh!*" Nona gave me a critical look. "Daphne has enough self-esteem issues to deal with. Dominic explained it all to me. He's very knowledgeable about animals."

"He told you to paint flowers on a cow?"

"Of course not." Nona laughed. "He suggested I weave ribbons in her tail. The flowers were my idea. And I'm using natural washable paints that have vitamins and a skin softener mixed in. My own creation."

"She's a cow, not a cover model. And Penny-Love will be here soon. How am I going to explained a flowered cow?"

"Tell her it's the latest in modern art."

I spread out my arms in frustration. "Why can't you be an ordinary grandmother who works in a garden or bakes homemade cookies?"

"There's a whole plate of homemade carob chip and asparagus cookies in the kitchen. Help yourself."

"Someone needs help," I muttered.

Daphne turned to moo at me, and I had a feeling I was being chastised.

Amazingly, when Penny-Love arrived, she didn't even notice the cow. But she didn't miss a muscle on Dominic's tanned, hard body.

"He's so hot!" Penny-Love pressed her face up against the window in my attic bedroom, peering down at Dominic as he repaired a broken fence board. "Do you have any binoculars?"

"No." I tugged on her arm. "Get away from the window, and I'll help you with your homework."

"He's wiping sweat off his brow. Now he's hammering again. Oops! He dropped a nail and is reaching for a new one. Thank you, gravity!"

"Pen, stop it."

"He's saying something to that wild bird perched on a fence post."

"Dominic calls the falcon Dagger."

"How sweet! I adore guys who like animals. It shows a deep sensitivity. Now he's petting the falcon. What a fantastic animal."

"The falcon or Dominic?" I couldn't resist asking. What was the big deal about Dominic anyway? Sure, he was good-looking if you went for the rugged, sweaty type. But he was also annoying and arrogant. Why couldn't Nona have mentored someone civilized, like Josh?

"Look!" Penny-Love said with her nose pressed against the window. "He's taking off his shirt. Have mercy! What a great set of abs! I'm in six-pack heaven! He's in way better shape than my last boyfriend. Let's go out and talk to him."

I shut my calculus book. "I want nothing to do with him."

"Anyone who looks that good can't be bad."

"Worse than bad. Don't say I didn't warn you."

Penny-Love glanced in the mirror over my dresser and smoothed her curly red hair, then flew out the door.

Sinking on my bed, I sighed. Then I reached out for a dish filled with lumpy, fresh-baked cookies and bit into an asparagus and carob chip cookie.

*   *   *

As I predicted, Dominic barely said one word to Penny before rudely striding off to the barn. But did that deter my boy-crazy friend? Not a bit. She invited herself to dinner and spent the whole time quizzing Nona about Dominic: Where was he from? What was his family like? Did he have a girlfriend?

"He's an excellent employee," Nona said evasively. "If you want to know more, you'll have to ask him."

But even though Penny-Love lingered after dinner, drying dishes while I washed, Dominic did not appear. We finished our homework, listened to CDs, and played computer games. Penny-Love kept glancing at the door while I kept a close watch on the clock. By nine-thirty, I was stressed completely. How could I tell my best friend to leave so I could rendezvous with Manny and Thorn?

Fortunately Penny-Love's cell phone rang at 9:35. I knew it was her mother before she answered. Her mother's angry voice came across loudly, "Why didn't you tell me you weren't going to be home for dinner? Why didn't you let me know where you were? I'm coming to get you, now!"

A subdued Penny-Love said goodbye, then hurried outside. I waited until her mother drove off before switching into dark clothes and finding a flashlight. I told Nona I needed to go copy some notes from a friend, and I crept outside and disappeared into the night.

18

Nona let me borrow her car, so it was just a quick drive to Taco Bell. A sliver of silvery moon shone through trees, exaggerating shadows into hidden threats. I kept having the urge to look around, as if someone were watching me.

It's just my imagination, I assured myself. Or was I sensing Opal? I always felt safer when she was nearby, a silent sentry watching over me. But when I tried to connect with her, I got nothing, and my uneasiness increased.

When I reached Taco Bell, I found Manny and Thorn waiting outside by a beat-up yellow station wagon.

"Hey, Beany." Manny's grin gleamed in the dark.

"You made it." Thorn sounded surprised, as if she'd expected me to bail.

"I told my grandmother I wouldn't be out long, so I hope this doesn't take long." I rubbed my sweaty hands on my jeans. "What's the plan?"

"That's what we're figuring out. I brought the complete list of stolen items," Manny said, withdrawing a folded paper from his trench coat. Yes—a trench coat, just like a B-movie detective.

Shining my flashlight on his paper, I skimmed the typed list. "Some of these things were taken by the janitor. At least that's what Opal told me."

"Opal?" Thorn raised her pierced brows. "Oh, your spirit guide."

"Everyone has one," I said a bit defensively. At least Thorn didn't seem to judge me, maybe because she knew what it was like to be judged.

Paper crinkled as Manny studied the list. "Mr. Watkins may have swiped a few office supplies. But what would he want with an engraved basketball trophy or the vice-principal's chair?"

"No wonder the Regis jocks were suspects," Thorn said, as we started walking toward the high school. "They've pulled pranks before—like putting a plastic shark in the swimming pool."

"With a fake human leg sticking out of the shark's mouth. The girls' swim team sure had a shock that day." Manny chuckled. "And the photo I took made a great front-page shot for the *Shout-Out*. But attacking the janitor wasn't a prank," he added. "And the Regis jocks had alibis."

"Alibis can be faked," I said as we cut through the school parking lot.

"But why call in an anonymous tip?" Manny asked.

"To stir things up?" Thorn said.

"Or throw suspicion on someone else." A creepy feeling came over me, and I glanced around at the silent building and the empty parking lot but didn't see anything unusual.

"Whatever. We need to get moving. You're on, Thorn." Manny held out the list to her. "Do your stuff."

The paper shimmered like a small ghost in the glow of Thorn's flashlight. She stared at it with a fierce concentration, energy surging around her in a stunning pink-yellow-white aura. I had the oddest sense of her flying up and going somewhere else. Not with her body, but with her soul. If I'd had any doubts about her ability, they quickly faded.

Thorn was more psychic than even she knew.

I could tell when Thorn returned. She blinked, disoriented, then gave a small shudder. Then she said simply, "Follow me."

She started walking, not toward the school as I'd expected, but the opposite direction, into dense woods beyond the school. She disappeared into shadowy trees with Manny, and I had to race to keep up. My feet crunched on brittle leaves and branches slapped my arms. I held tight to my flashlight; its slim beam bounced off tree trunks and uneven ground.

We hurried over weeds, around rocks, avoiding holes, deeper and deeper into gloomy woods. When we reached a thick wall of berry bushes bordering a rushing creek, we couldn't go any further.

Thorn untangled a spindly branch, but it sprang back and slapped her. "Stupid bushes! We can't stop now."

"But the path ends here," Manny said. "There's no way through."

"There has to be," Thorn said with fierce determination. "We have to keep going."

"It'll take a machete, and I left mine in the trunk."

"We'll just have to find another path," Thorn said, clearly resolved on getting through. "I'll look toward the right."

"Okay." Manny nodded. "And I'll go left."

"Hey guys, what about me?" I asked, but they were already hurrying off separately. And I noticed my flashlight's beam seemed fainter. Clouds hid the moon and the sky grew darker. I thought longingly of my nightlights and my cozy, safe room. Why had I agreed to this anyway? No one had connected me to the vandalism, so I was in the clear. But if I were caught tonight, everything would be ruined.

I waited in the dark, listening intently for Thorn and Manny. Nearby, a bush rustled. I jumped back with a startled cry. Hugging myself, I shone my flashlight in a wide circle. Night closed around me with fluttering birds, croaking frogs, and a soft whisper of wind in the dry leaves. The sound grew nearer, and I clenched my flashlight. Branches shifted, golden eyes flashed in blackness, and there stood a dark figure silently watching with a bird perched on his shoulder.

"Dominic!" I exclaimed as the figure vanished. Gone so quickly, I was still staring, sure I'd imagined the whole thing.

"Sabine!" Manny's footsteps pounded through brush as he rushed over. "I heard you yell. Are you okay?"

"I'm not sure." I swallowed hard. "I think I saw—"

"What?"

"I don't know. It was so fast, I'm not sure what I saw. It's gone now anyway."

"Probably a raccoon. Bet you scared it more than it scared you."

"You'd lose that bet." My flashlight flickered, then went completely out.

"Looks like you need new batteries. Stick close to me and you won't get lost." He patted my shoulder. "We'll head back as soon as we find Thorn—"

As he spoke her name, Thorn's voice rang out, "Manny! Sabine!"

"She's found something." Manny grabbed my hand. "Come on!"

We found Thorn crouched on the ground by a pile of brush. When Manny shone his flashlight on the pile, something glinted from underneath dead branches.

"It's metal," I said.

Manny pulled away branches. "The vice principal's chair!"

"But what's it doing out here?" Thorn wondered.

"Highly suspicious." Branches crackled and snapped as Manny yanked out the chair. "Why would anyone break into the school, attack the janitor, then drag a chair way out in the woods?"

I agreed it was strange, but I was more curious about what wasn't there. "Where's the other stuff?"

"A definite hole in this puzzle." Manny shook his head. "I don't know."

"I—I do," Thorn said in an odd dazed voice. She touched the spiked dog collar around her neck and stared off with a glazed expression.

Then she whirled around and ran back toward the school.

Manny and I didn't hesitate and took off after her. Thorn's clunky boots crashed through the woods. I followed behind Manny, holding on his arm so I wouldn't get lost. At first I felt like I was running in a black tunnel, but trees thinned and we were out of the woods, racing across the grassy sports field and past the bleachers rising like sleepy dragons in the dark. Thorn was a blur ahead of us, sprinting across blacktop, turning a corner and stopping at a closed door.

"We need to get inside the school," Thorn said urgently. "But the doors are locked."

"I know a way," Manny said. "A door with a faulty lock—all it takes is a swift kick in the right spot."

One stride of Manny's seemed to equal two of mine—

math that added up to exhaustion. I pushed myself faster, panting and growing more anxious with each step, worries pounding through my head. What if the janitor's attacker came back? What if the new janitor caught us? What if Nona got worried and called the police? What if my legs collapsed and I passed out?

Manny led us through a side door by the cafeteria, then Thorn rushed ahead. Manny hurried after her, catching up as she made a sharp right at a bank of lockers. Feeling dizzy, I leaned against a wall until my head cleared. The eerie glow from the security lights made the hallway seem both familiar and alien.

As I turned the corner, I saw Thorn staring at some lockers. "Look," she was telling Manny.

"Why'd you stop here?" My heart pounded from effort.

"Because the missing stuff is here." Thorn pointed. "Whoever owns this locker is our thief."

"But that's impossible!" I gasped trying to catch my breath.

"Why?" Manny asked.

"This is my locker."

19

Someone dangerous was out to get me.

That was the only thing I knew for certain. No matter how hard I tried to summon a name or visualize this faceless person, I got nothing. And apprehension crept into my soul.

It was Thorn's idea to remove the basketball trophy, staplers, and other stolen stuff from my locker and leave them with the chair in the woods. Manny agreed right away, and I was so touched at their concern for me that I didn't know how to thank them.

"No prob," Manny said with a wicked grin. "Always happy to transport stolen goods for a friend."

Despite everything else that could go wrong, nothing did. The substitute janitor never even saw us—although we spotted him sleeping in the teacher's lounge. It was almost midnight by the time I reached home.

Lights glowed from within the house, a good sign Nona was still busy at her computer. When she closed in on a perfect match, she lived in another reality. If I interrupted her, she'd look at me like I was a stranger. She felt so guilty after this happened a few times that now she did most of her work late in the evening.

A flap of wings made me glance up. Caught in the glare from the porch light, a solitary bird glided low in a silent flight across the pasture. The bird circled over the barn, then swooped down and disappeared through an open barn window. Footsteps on gravel made me turn. In the dim light from the chicken coop, I could see a slim, muscular figure.

I hadn't imagined it—Dominic had followed me.

Instead of being afraid, I was angry. It was bad enough someone was out to get me at school; I didn't have to put up with this crap at home.

"Dominic!" I shouted. "You are such a jerk!"

He stopped by the barn and slowly turned toward me.

I strode over, fuming. "You followed me tonight." I stabbed my finger at his chest. "Don't deny it."

"I won't." He faced me; his blue eyes were narrowed and far from friendly.

"Why'd you do it?"

"To help."

"Help?" I snorted. "Like I believe that."

"I don't care what you believe," he said with disgust. "I was wrong about you."

"What's that supposed to mean?"

"How could you let Nona down like this? Did you do it for the thrill? To show off to your friends?"

"Huh?" I scrunched my forehead. "Do what?"

"Steal." He spat out the word.

"But I didn't!"

"You had those things in your locker, then you hid them in the woods."

His words slammed into me. "It's not what you think."

"What else can I think? I know what I saw." Sadness hooded his eyes as he looked at me. Dagger shrieked from the loft, and Dominic turned and started toward the barn.

"Wait!" I called.

He paused. "Why should I?"

"Because we both care about Nona. I don't owe you any answers, but I'll tell you anyway." I glanced at the soft light still shining from my grandmother's office. "Only not out here."

"Inside then." He led me into the barn.

Bales of hay climbed to the ceiling on half of the large wood-floored building, and a cow mooed from one of the stalls lining the opposite wall. Dominic moved toward the staircase, flipping on a light that illuminated a flight of steep stairs. My heartbeat quickened as I climbed.

Entering Dominic's private loft apartment felt like stepping into the enemy camp. I didn't even like him, so it shouldn't matter what he thought. Yet it did, and I felt compelled to set him straight.

As I stood uneasily on an old braided rug, Dagger fluttered on a wooden post by an open window. Except for some candles and crystals on a dresser, there were no photographs, books, or knick-knacks. There was little evidence of Dominic's personality, as if he'd locked himself away in secrecy and hidden the key.

"Make it quick," Dominic said sarcastically, mimicking my own bitchy tone of a few days earlier, when he was in my room.

"Someone put those things in my locker. I was framed."

"Why would anyone do that?"

"I have no idea." I sank into a chair. "I wish I did."

"Can't you figure it out?" he asked, pulling up a stool across from me. "With your powers?"

"Don't you think I've tried? But I never can get visions about myself. It's scary knowing someone hates me. If it happened at my last school, I'd understand. But people here don't know about my ... my abilities."

"Are you sure?"

"I've only told Manny and Thorn."

"And you trust them?"

"Yeah. Tonight they came through for me in a big way. But I'm not so sure about you." I regarded him suspiciously. "How did you know I was at the school?"

"A friend told me."

"Who? Not Penny-Love?"

He turned away and walked over to his falcon.

"Is it someone I know?"

"Maybe, but not exactly."

"You're not making any sense." I studied him, trying to pick up on his aura, but his colors were as nondescript as his room. I concentrated on his energy.

The room faded out, and I was suddenly outside in a drizzling, icy rain that sliced into my skin. My stomach ached with a raw emptiness. Hunger. And when I looked down, I saw a shackle chained to my leg. No, not my leg. A scrawny young boy in bloody jeans. Rain whipped against his frail, battered body, and he huddled against a tree trunk. There was a hollow anguished sound, more animal than human, coming from the boy. So much pain, too much to bear.

As quickly as it came, the vision passed. I sucked in a breath and grabbed on to his dresser to steady my trembling legs.

"I'm so sorry," was all I could say.

"What for?" he demanded. "Something just happened, didn't it? What did you see?"

"A boy." My heart ached. "Chained outside in the rain—like an animal. He was starving and cold and scared. And he—he was you."

His expression hardened. "You don't know anything."

"Do you want to talk about it?"

"No. It was a long time ago."

"But the pain is still there."

"Forget about it." His brow furrowed. "Don't waste sympathy on that boy—he survived."

"Who—who did that to him, to you?"

"An uncle." Dominic's eyes glinted dangerously. "A sick person who felt powerful if he was beating on someone smaller than him. He eventually got what he deserved, and I realized I'd had more power than him all along."

"What power? I know Nona invited you here because you have some sort of psychic ability."

"I'm not psychic."

"Then what are you?"

"A communicator—but not with ghosts or people."

"What's left?"

"Can't you guess? Lillybelle warned me you were going out tonight."

"My cat?"

"Yeah." He slid his hand across Dagger's silky feathers.

"You can communicate with—" it shouldn't have shocked me, but it did.

"—with animals. Yeah, I can," he said.

20

The next morning I awoke from a strange dream where Dominic stepped out of the pages of my childhood collection of Dr. Dolittle books. Only instead of being pudgy and middle-aged, Dominic was a young, hunky animal doctor, and I was the mythical two-headed llama called a Push-Me-Pull-You. Dominic pulled me in one direction, while Josh pulled me in another. I couldn't remember the details, but when I woke up, I ached all over.

It was tempting to ignore my clock alarm because that meant going to school—where I had an unknown enemy.

A lavender fragrance and soft breeze stirred my blankets, despite my closed window. Peering around my room, I whispered, "Opal?"

Good morning, my dear Sabine.

"It's not that good of a morning. I want to stay in bed and hide. Everything's so confusing—can you help?"

I do hope so—helping you is my avowed mission and fervent goal.

"Then tell me why somebody put stolen stuff in my locker."

You already know the answer, if you trust your instincts and examine the situation.

"But I don't know anything! I had those visions about Danielle and tried to help her, which got me into worse trouble."

These troubles will seem insignificant in the fullness of time. If I gave you the answers, that would cheat you out of valuable life experiences and cheating is always wrong. The truest answers lie in the test.

So this was some kind of test, I realized—then groaned. I hated tests. But a flash of insight hit me, and I understood why someone might target me. "Was that stuff put in my locker because I'm trying to find the vandals?"

Vandal, she corrected. *Singular.*

"Is it someone I know?"

We all know each other at some level. Examine all relationships closely and set something right to avoid tragic consequences.

"Why do you always talk like a fortune cookie? Can't you just give me a name?"

No, she replied in that maddening literal tone.

"Then how will I find out?"

Enlightenment appears in many forms.

"And your point is?" I asked sarcastically.

You were blessed with a clever mind that is in sore need of critical use. Don't assume watching you muddle through your journey is a slice of sunshine. Not even—as you like to say. You frustrate me to the ends of Jupiter! Nevertheless, you are making excellent progress, and I have confidence in you.

"Gee, thanks," I grumbled as her energy pulled away to return to spirit-land or wherever she hung out when she wasn't nagging me.

*　　*　　*

As I was rinsing off my cereal dish and putting it in the dishwasher, Penny-Love showed up. I was surprised she'd come way down our driveway instead of waiting for me on the street. But one look at her snug, sheer top over a new pair of jeans and I connected the romantic dots. She'd even taken the time to iron the kinks out of her red hair so it fell in a long, silky wave around her shoulders.

"Is Dominic around?" she asked coyly.

"No."

"Too bad, but there's always after school. Is it okay if I come over again?"

"Of course. You don't have to ask."

"Good!" Penny-Love said with a bounce in her step as we left the house and started down the driveway. "I came up with the perfect way to get Dominic to notice me. He's into birds, right?"

"Actually all animals."

"Which includes birds, so I'm going to tell him my canary is sick and ask him to come over to look at it."

"You don't have a canary."

"Details, details." Penny-Love waved away my words. "When I want something—or someone—nothing stops me."

"Why would you want Dominic?" I asked, hoping to talk some sense into her. "He's rude and likes animals better than people. I can't see how you'd want a grump like him when you could have any guy at school."

"Except Josh," she said teasingly.

"Right." I smiled at his name.

We were laughing as we reached the school. Waving goodbye, I headed for my locker, eager to see Josh. Only when I neared the lockers, it was too crowded to find anyone. Students and even a few teachers were gawking at something.

A locker banged and bodies shifted, and I saw Dunlap. Moving closer, I saw the principal in conversation with an olive-skinned custodian I didn't recognize. The custodian wielded some kind of tool or maybe a key. He opened a locker, slammed it shut, then opened another.

I stared in horror, afraid to breathe and give myself away.

Locker 124. Closing in on mine. They wouldn't find any-thing more than books, a sweater, and a half-eaten Snickers bar—but last night they would have found plenty.

Shaking inside, I whirled around—and smacked into a dark-haired girl with a dragonfly tattoo on her wrist.

"Danielle!" I exclaimed. "Sorry, I wasn't looking."

"I was coming to talk to you." Her face was tear-streaked and her voice cracked as she added, "I don't know what else to do."

"What is it?" My thoughts flew back to Sunday night. "Did the police find out about us?"

"No, nothing like that. No one even questioned me. It's—It's Evan."

"Oh." I let out the breath I'd been holding. "Is he okay?"

"Yeah, but I'm not. He—" She broke off with a sob.

"What is it?" I put my arm gently around her.

"He dumped me!"

"Oh, I'm so sorry." I wasn't really, but I couldn't admit that. I tried to summon some sincerity.

"I love him more than my own life. I'd do anything for him—anything at all—except let him go. But he doesn't want me."

"It's his loss," I soothed. "You'll find someone better."

"There is no one better. "

No one better at being self-centered and arrogant, I thought.

I led Danielle over to a bench and tried to calm her down. "I don't know much about love. Uh…This will seem insignificant in the fullness of time." I wanted to bite back my words when I realized I'd repeated what Opal had told me. "I mean, you'll be okay."

"Not without him. You have no idea what it's like—how much it hurts without him. Like bleeding on the inside." Tears slipped down her cheeks. "I feel all panicky, like I'm falling apart. I *need* Evan."

"You only need yourself," I insisted. "Give it some time, you'll get over him."

"Never!" She clutched at my arm; her eyes were wild. "You've got to help me. Josh will listen to you and Evan will listen to Josh. Get Josh to convince Evan to take me back."

"I can't ask Josh something like that."

"But Evan loves me, I know he does. He just has a lot of needs and I let him down. But I can try harder, if he'll just give me the chance." Her voice cracked, and she looked ready to collapse. "Talk to Josh. I'm begging you!"

"Danielle—I can't…" my words trailed off as I shook my head.

"I'm desperate. Please, please!"

I hesitated, remembering the vision of a bloody dragon-fly. Danielle was like a frightened child and the vision tied me to her in a way I didn't understand. Yet I couldn't turn her down, even if that meant reuniting her with Evan.

"Okay," I said reluctantly.

"Thank you! Thank you!" She hugged me, then whirled around and left.

Barely a minute later, Josh showed up.

*   *   *

Josh was outraged when he realized my locker had been searched.

"That's unconstitutional!" he ranted as we walked to our first class. "I can't believe you allowed this to take place without protesting. They had no right to invade your privacy."

"The lockers are school property; we're just borrowing them."

"But the things inside are your personal belongings."

I'd never seen Josh so worked up, and I was secretly pleased he was acting protective. Like a hero coming to the aid of his lady. I wasn't about to spoil this moment by bringing up Danielle.

"A lot of lockers were searched," I pointed out. "Not just mine."

"That doesn't make it okay," Josh insisted. "You should call a lawyer."

"What sixteen-year-old has a lawyer?"

"A smart one. If the school pulls more stunts like this, I may get one."

By the end of our first class, Josh had calmed down, but only after I agreed to let him write a letter of protest on my behalf to the school board.

When we met at lunch, he had the letter composed in a spiral notebook and couldn't wait to show it to me. I tried—I really tried—to bring up the topic of Danielle and Evan, but it just didn't happen.

That afternoon, a news flash rippled through the school. Stolen items were found hidden in the woods. No one could figure out why the stuff had been dumped in the woods. Rumors placed the blame on the Regis High kids, again. But no one really cared anymore.

With the missing things recovered, there was a sense of closure, and by tomorrow it would be old news.

Except to me.

Someone had invaded my locker, and I couldn't forget that. The lock hadn't been forced, so either someone picked it or knew the combination. But I'd only revealed it to two people: Josh and Penny-Love.

When Penny-Love came over to my house later, I asked her if she'd told the combination to anyone else.

"How can you even ask such a thing? I'm mortally wounded!"

"Sorry," I said, ignoring the melodrama. "But with all that commotion about lockers being searched, I guess I'm a little paranoid."

"Your combination is safe with me." She moved away from the window where she'd been spying on Dominic. "I've never told another person. And I keep it safely written on a Post-It in my locker."

"You *wrote it down?*" I exclaimed.

"Well, sure. I have so many numbers to remember,

I have to write them down or my brain sinks in number soup."

"So you left my combo in the same locker you let your cheerleading friends use because it's closer to the gym? The same locker you shared with your last two boyfriends? The same locker you left wide open for a full day last week because you were in a hurry?"

She nodded, and I groaned.

I might as well have announced my combination in the *Sheridan Shout-Out*.

*　　*　　*

Saturday morning, when Josh showed up for our date, I didn't recognize him. And who could blame me? He came to the door wearing a rainbow shaggy wig, floppy chicken feet, and a green nose.

"Squeeze my nose," was the first thing he said when he saw me—not exactly the romantic words a girl wants to hear.

"Won't that hurt?"

"Nah. Give my nose a big squeeze."

Feeling kind of dumb, I reached out and pinched his plastic nose. *Squawk!* The nose erupted with a thundered honk and fake snot dribbled out of the green nostrils. "Lovely."

"It's just fake slime." When he laughed, more snot oozed from his nose. "Kids love it!"

"Ha ha," I said, staring with disgust at the green gunk

on my fingers. Then I hurried to the bathroom and scrubbed my hands.

On the way to Valley General Hospital, we received strange looks from other drivers on the road. Hadn't they ever seen a clown driving? Instead of being embarrassed, I found myself grinning. Josh was such a wonderful mix of silly and serious. And underneath all the greasepaint and fake snot, he was one gorgeous guy who—amazingly—cared about me.

At the hospital, I was impressed by how many people greeted Josh. Nurses, doctors, patients, and even maintenance workers. In floppy clown clothes where no one could even see his face, he was loved.

Especially by the kids.

He sang goofy songs, picking up a broom and strumming it like a guitar. Then, instead of pulling a rabbit out of a hat, he pulled Silly String and stuffed toys out of a bedpan. Kids in wheelchairs, connected to IVs, and wrapped in bandages laughed and begged him for more. It was great.

I hadn't completely forgotten my promise to Danielle, but finding the right moment to talk to Josh about it wasn't exactly easy. I didn't want to distract him from his performance. So I waited until we were on our way back home from the hospital.

"I saw Danielle yesterday," I finally said, holding the rainbow wig he'd tossed aside. "Has Evan said anything about her?"

"Nah." Josh shook his head. "He's seeing a new girl—Shelby."

"Shelby McIntire?" I had a mental picture of a stunning girl with honey-blond hair and shining dark eyes.

"Yeah. You know her?"

"Not personally, but she's a cheerleader and gorgeous." I sighed. "Poor Danielle. She's devastated."

"Evan's girls always get over him."

"I'm not so sure about Danielle. She's seems fragile. She totally fell apart over some test. She was really freaked out when I saw her."

"Don't worry. Danielle will be fine. I probably shouldn't say this, but I think Evan broke it off because she's too brainy. His ego probably couldn't take it."

"She's smart?"

"Yeah, didn't you know? She's got a photographic memory and always aces tests. She helped Evan improve his grades and stay on the football team."

"Then he dumped her."

"Evan can be harsh with girls."

"So why do you stay friends with him?"

"He's okay when you get to know him. And I've known him for a long time. He and my brother and I were practically inseparable... and after the accident, Evan was there for me."

"Well. That's okay," I said begrudgingly, thinking how much I valued Nona's unwavering support of me. That kind of loyalty was rare. Not many people could be counted on when things got tough.

Josh slowed the car and parked in my driveway. He shut off the motor then turned to me. "I think it's cool you're concerned about Danielle—it's part of what makes you special."

Naturally, after that, we didn't talk about Danielle or Evan anymore.

It wasn't until I was climbing into bed that night that I mentally replayed our conversation and realized something startling.

If Danielle had a photographic memory, why would she worry about taking a test? She had no reason to steal a key and break into private teacher files.

What had she really been looking for?

21

Josh had to go to a family dinner, so he dropped me off early. Since there was still a few hours of daylight left, I found Danielle's address in the phone book and took off on my bike to talk with her.

When I'd first moved to Sheridan Valley, wallowing in a dark mood of disgrace, I'd felt stranded. Sure, it was just thirty minutes to Sacramento or Stockton, but I was used to the bustling pace of San Jose. And at first I didn't have any friends, so I spent a lot of time reading under a shady willow—until Nona gave me an old bike and ordered me to get out. It was scary at first, but after a few days of exploring, I felt an empowering sense of freedom. Free to fly into the wind, away from the past.

The upscale development Danielle lived in, Summit Estates, backed up against the far side of our woods. I turned left onto Maple Street, passed a walnut orchard, and rode until fields gave way to pristine new homes. Addresses weren't displayed on the houses, but were uniformly painted in gold lettering below the sidewalks. Danielle's sprawling tri-level home had a circular driveway winding through lush manicured shrubs. I smoothed my tousled blond hair and tucked in my T-shirt, then knocked on the door.

Only I was five minutes too late.

Danielle's father told me she just left to watch her boyfriend's football practice.

Boyfriend? Did she already have a new guy or had she gotten back with Evan? I wondered, hiding my surprise with a polite thank-you. A minute later, I was back on my bike, heading for Sheridan High.

*   *   *

Shouts mingled with the thud of crashing bodies as I neared the football field. Propping my bike against a fence, I walked around the bleachers, looking for Danielle. I finally spotted her sitting in a far corner of the top bleacher, her raven hair tucked under a cap that concealed most of her face. She was so intent on watching the field, she didn't notice me until I came up beside her.

"Sabine!" She jumped in her seat. "Don't sneak up on me like that!"

"Sorry. What are you doing here, anyway?"

"None of your business."

"Why are you spying on Evan?"

"It's not illegal to watch practice."

"But why put yourself through this?" I shook my head at her sadly. "You have to get over him, Danielle."

"He's still my boyfriend. We're just having some problems."

"And I have a problem with being lied to." I took a seat next to her and shot her an accusing look. "Why did you really sneak into the supply room?"

"I already told you." Her too-large cap slipped off of her head, and when she picked it up, the tiny tattooed dragonfly on her wrist seemed to darken.

"Josh told me about your photographic memory."

"You talked to Josh?" She clutched my arm. "Did he say anything about Evan? Is he going to help us get back together?"

I ignored the questions and fired back, "Why were you in that supply room?"

"To copy a bio test."

"Danielle! The truth!"

"But it is the truth, except—" she gnawed on her thumbnail, then added in a whisper, "except the test wasn't for me."

"Then who was it—Ohmygod! Evan! You did it for

him?" I glanced out at the field to where Evan was running with the ball.

"His bio teacher hates jocks, and Evan will get kicked off the football team if he flunks another test."

"So you tried to steal a test."

"Only I couldn't find it, then you came, the janitor caught us, and everything was messed up."

"The janitor was messed up more after we left. Did you see anyone suspicious?"

"No," she said a bit too quickly.

There was a roar from the other players and people in the stands as Evan did something impressive down on the field. The coach slapped Evan on the back, then gestured for the players to huddle up.

Danielle stared across the field, longingly, her hands coming together to clap softly. "Isn't he wonderful? I miss him so much. I can hardly stand it. I let him down and now he won't talk to me. If I can just get him alone and explain, everything will be fine again."

"After the way he treated you? Why would you want him back?"

"We're soul mates, and we'll love each other forever. Just wait—next time you see me, we'll be together."

I frowned, unsure what to say. I could feel in my gut that Danielle and Evan were a bad combination, yet it wasn't fair to judge them. Maybe Evan was different when he was alone with Danielle. Josh thought he was a good guy, so he couldn't be a total jerk.

Whooping and stomping jerked my attention back to football practice. Hulking guys were high-fiving as the coach pumped them up with a pep talk.

I watched Danielle, wondering if she would go to Evan. But it was a different girl who ran across the field and threw herself on Evan—a petite girl with streaked, honey-blond hair. Evan dropped his helmet and opened his arms to sweep her up in a hug. She was so tiny that her feet left the ground when Evan twirled her around.

Danielle groaned, slumping back down to the bench.

"I'm so sorry," I said softly.

She stared across the field, tears spilling down her cheeks.

I took her shaking hands in mine. "Don't let him get to you."

She didn't say a word and had turned as pale as a corpse. She didn't object when I led her down the bleachers. But then she just stopped and stared at the ground.

"How could he?" she murmured, as if stunned.

"He does it all the time. Some kids call him 'Moving On, Marsh.'"

"But it was different with us. He said I wasn't like the other girls. That he—he loved me." Her expression changed from ice to fire. "I hate him!"

"Good—he deserves it."

"I—I wish he were dead."

"He isn't worth the cost of a hit man." I joked nervously, startled by this hostile change in her. It was like her emotions had been pushed to the edge, and she was in danger of falling. "Come on, you need to get out of here."

"It doesn't matter. Nothing matters anymore—except getting even." Her hands tightened into fists. "If I can't have him, no one can."

I reached out to put my arms around her, but she shook me off.

"He has no right to treat me like this! Do you know what I *did* for him? More than studying—I *did* his homework," she said angrily. "Then I broke into the school and almost got arrested! All for him!"

"You're through with him now—he can't hurt you anymore."

"Oh, I hurt all right. But he's going to hurt worse."

"Let it go," I said, unnerved by her viciousness. "Revenge never solves anything."

"He's going to be sorry he betrayed me because I know enough to ruin him."

"What do you mean?"

"You want to know what really happened at the school that night? I only told you half of the story. You were right. I was lying—to protect him. I didn't go there alone—he made me go there, and he waited outside."

"Evan was there?"

"Yes." She grimaced as if tasting something bitter. "It was all his idea. He begged me to find the test and memorize it. I was thrilled to do something so important for him, sure he'd love me more than ever. Only, you know what happened when I came back after I ditched you?"

I shook my head.

"He yelled at me. Called me a loser and blamed me for screwing up. When I said I loved him, he just laughed and told me to get lost."

"What did you do?"

"I left. But Evan didn't." She paused, turning around to glare towards the football field. "Last I saw of him that night, he was headed back to the school to get the test."

22

Players were leaving the field, and, when Danielle spotted Evan and Shelby among the group, she threw up her hands and cried, "I have to go!" Then she took off, leaving me standing there, stunned by what she'd revealed.

Slowly I walked away, trying to figure out what to do. How could I make a serious accusation against Josh's best friend? I didn't know for sure what he'd done that night. Had Evan copied the test? Was he still planning to cheat? Had he witnessed the vandalism? Or had he taken part in it?

I didn't like Evan much, but would he trash his own school? He was a cheater, not a vandal, I thought. Maybe he'd just seen what happened and was afraid to come forward.

Or maybe Danielle lied—again.

Grabbing my bike by the handlebars, I started to leave, when I felt a tap on my shoulder. Whirling around, I found myself face to chest with a tall football player. "Evan!"

He flashed a lazy grin. "Don't act so happy to see me. What were you doing here? Checking up on me?"

"No." I propped my bike back against the fence. "Why would you think that?"

"It's no secret you're not a fan of football—or me," he added accusingly. "Josh has been different since hooking up with you. I hardly see him anymore."

"He's busy, I guess."

"Don't try to interfere in our friendship. No girl has ever come between us."

"And there have been plenty of girls," I couldn't resist saying sarcastically. "I saw you out on the field with your new girlfriend. Where'd she go?"

"Some babysitting job." He narrowed his gaze at me. "And I saw you—with Danielle."

"She left. I'm leaving, too." I stepped away from him, eager to get on my bike and leave.

"Wait!" He shifted around to block my way. "What did Danielle tell you about me?"

"Nothing."

"Sure about that?"

"Well, she was upset about Shelby. I see you're living up to your reputation."

"What's wrong with moving on when things don't work out? That doesn't make me a bad guy."

"Depends on why they didn't work out."

"Josh wouldn't judge me without hearing my side first."

"He always sees the best in people, and I admire that about him, but I'm not as trusting. Not that my opinion matters—this is between you and Danielle."

"We're over. I'm with Shelby now, and she's nothing like Danielle—she knows how to treat a guy right."

"Does that include stealing—" I slapped my hand over my big mouth. Then I glanced at my watch as if I'd just remembered a late appointment. "I have to go."

"Wait." He seemed to grow taller and wider as he blocked my way. "Obviously Danielle told you some lies and you've jumped to the wrong conclusion."

"I really have to leave."

"She told you about the test. Didn't she? Which means she also told you we were at the school last Sunday."

"I don't know what you're talking about." I stepped to the side, only he slid right back in front of me.

His smile never faltered—like he was toying with me—and he even casually waved at some kids who passed. "If you wanna know what really went down that night, don't rush off. I'll tell you something I haven't told anyone."

"What?"

"I have a picture of the dude who trashed the school, caught in the act. So, do you want to hear my side now?"

I didn't trust him, yet how could I walk away from this? A picture! Real proof! Manny would be totally blown away. So I nodded.

"I'm ashamed I tried to cheat." Evan's sincerity seemed genuine as we walked toward the school. "But when Danielle found out I was going to be kicked off the team if I flunked another science test, she offered to copy the test, and I couldn't talk her out of it. So I went along and kept watch outside."

Obviously not a close watch or the janitor wouldn't have caught us, I thought. Then I wondered, does he know I was there, too?

"I was keeping a low profile and saw this guy sneaking around. He was carrying a spraypaint can, acting real suspicious. I couldn't call the cops because Danielle could get in trouble. But I have one of those cell phones that takes pictures, and I took his."

"Why didn't you get Danielle out of there and call the police?"

"I wasn't sure what he was up to at first. It wasn't till the next day that I knew what went down." Then he hung his head and added quietly, "Sorry if I came on strong at first, but Danielle gets to me."

"You're the one who dumped her."

"I felt bad about that. I was really into her until she

started talking crazy, making all these threats about killing herself, me, and anyone I ever dated."

"She was just hurt."

"So was I." He sighed dramatically. "Come on—I printed the picture out and hid it somewhere safe, just in case I needed it."

I folded my arms across my chest, not sure whether to believe him or not. It all seemed so polished and convenient. But I did want to see the picture. So making sure my bike was locked, I followed him toward the school. I walked quickly, glancing nervously over my shoulder.

Sabine, came a mental whisper. Opal. It was just like her to butt in when I was finding answers on my own. So I shut her out by visualizing Manny's reaction when I showed him the vandal's picture. He'd be way impressed—especially when I revealed I hadn't had any help from the other side.

As we neared the same unlocked door that Manny had used to get into the school, Evan paused to look around.

"Did you hear that?" he asked, glancing around uneasily.

"What? No one's around."

"You never know who's watching," he said ominously.

Why was Evan acting like this? A prickly feeling made me look over my shoulder again, and I glimpsed quick movement in a tree-filled courtyard. Only a bird or squirrel, I assured myself. Still, my heart pounded as I walked with Evan into the hushed, dimly lit building. With the school shut down for the weekend, the halls seemed eerily quiet.

"With all the locker searches, I didn't trust leaving the picture in my locker. Since I still had the key Danielle used to get into the storage room, I hid the picture in here."

Evan stopped at the supply room where I'd found Danielle. He dropped his backpack and reached into his pocket for the key. He opened the door and made a gentlemanly sweep of his arm. "Ladies first."

I froze, remembering the last time I'd been here—caught by the janitor. Had it only been a week ago? Glancing inside, I saw nothing threatening: a desk, chairs, and file cabinets. Yet something felt very wrong.

"I don't know about—" I started to say, only a vicious shove from behind knocked my breath away.

Gasping, I tumbled forward, falling hard onto the concrete floor. Pain shot through my knees, the door slammed, and the room went dark. It happened so fast. Before I could jump up to rush at the door, there was a sharp click of the door locking behind me.

Pounding my fists, I screamed, "Let me out!"

Evan just laughed. "Scream all you want," he said through the door. "The janitor can't hear you. He's picking up trash by the football field."

"You jerk!" My knees stung, but I ignored the pain as I yanked and rattled the knob. It wouldn't budge. "Why are you doing this?"

"Damage control—and it's kind of fun."

"I'll damage you when I get out of here!"

"So naïve," he taunted. "You really believed I had a picture?"

"No picture? Then why did you—" My body stiffened but my brain whirled. "You put that stuff in my locker! Why target me? What did I ever do to you?"

"Come between me and Josh. He's always looked up to me like a big brother, but he wouldn't listen about you. I suspected when I met you that you were trouble. And I knew it for sure when you started hanging around Danielle, getting her to tell you things about me."

"So you set me up?"

"I knew your locker combination from watching Josh. It was a brilliant move, shifting the blame on you. I've been trying to figure out how to show Josh you're not right for him. He'll be upset when he finds out you're a thief, but I'll be there for him. He'll listen to me in the future before he dates some nobody."

My mind continued to grind out the details, not fully comprehending what Evan was saying. "You called in the anonymous tip!" I smacked the door harder, wishing it were his face.

"Clever, huh? Only, somehow, you got lucky and found the stuff before Dunlap searched the lockers."

"Wait till I get out of here! I'll tell him everything."

"Try it. Think he'll believe you over his star football player? My team will cover for me, say I was with them, so it'll be your word against mine. And no one will trust you by then. Including Josh."

Panicked, I balled my hands into fists and pounded harder. "Open up! Now!"

"Keep making noise. When the custodian finishes the football field, he'll let you out. Only he's not going to be very happy when he sees what you've done."

"I haven't done anything!"

"No one's gonna believe that." A strong odor wafted through the crack at the bottom of the door. Paint! And Evan laughed in a cold way that made me shudder. "By Monday morning the whole school will know who the vandal is. You."

23

Trapped. And the only hope of a rescue would result in my being blamed for crimes I didn't commit. Why had I been dumb enough to believe Evan? He'd called me naïve, and he was right. I knew he was a jerk and had never liked him. Yet I'd followed him anyway.

My eyes watered from paint fumes and rubbing them only made them sting. Sinking with hopelessness, I whispered into the darkness, "What am I going to do? Opal, why didn't you warn me?"

I tried to, she sassed back. *Only you chose not to listen.*

"Shout next time." I sagged against the door. "Not that there'll ever be a next time. Evan is arranging an alibi while I'm waiting to be caught. The janitor will think I was stupid enough to lock myself in after spraying graffiti and no one will believe it was Evan. Everyone will turn against me. I'll have to leave school… and Josh."

Such negativity is unbecoming for a young lady. In my day, I was too consumed with exhausting chores to give thought to my own comfort. You need to worry less about trifles and focus on the larger picture. Wallowing in self-pity will accomplish nothing. Seek a positive action.

"News flash: I'm stuck in here. Can't do squat."

Are you sure about that?

I started to argue, but when her energy pulled back, I knew it was useless. What did she know anyway? Safe in spirit-land where you could bet doors were never locked.

Still, she was right. I couldn't give up.

My eyes were beginning to adjust and I explored the room, feeling the wall for a light switch. I remembered that the janitor had reached up for an overhead bulb. Within seconds, my black hole of despair flooded with light.

Now all I needed was an open door.

In movies, locks were jimmied open with credit cards or hairpins. I was too young for a credit card and the scrunchie around my ponytail was the closest I had to a hairpin. I started searching the room, checking drawers that weren't locked. I found pencils, pens, paper, rubber bands, paper-clips and tape. Unbending a large paperclip, I tried poking it in the lock—but no luck. So I searched again—then shrieked with joy when I found a screwdriver.

Forget the lock, I'd unhinge the whole damn door.

Like the rest of the school, the door was old. The hinge was held on by a few screws. My knees ached as I kneeled on the floor and set to work. I pressed my arm against the door for leverage. As the first screw began to turn, I heard a noise from outside in the hall.

Please, not the janitor so soon! I needed more time!

The knob jiggled and turned. The door swung open, and I saw—

"Dominic! Am I glad to see you!"

"Well, that's a first." He flashed a wry smile, showing dimples that softened his rugged face. "You okay?"

"Yeah. How'd you know I was in trouble?" I thought of the shadow I'd seen earlier by a tree. "Oh, don't tell me—a little bird told you."

"A big bird," he said, looking around curiously. "How'd you get locked in?"

"Evan did it." I could tell by Dominic's puzzled expression that he didn't recognize the name. I returned the screwdriver to the drawer then said hastily, "I'll explain later. Let's get out of here."

Once in the hall, the smell of paint was overpowering. A very rude message was scrawled on a wall above an insulting drawing of Principal Dunlap sitting on a giant cowboy hat that resembled a toilet.

Dominic touched the wall, then glanced at the blue smear on his finger. "Fresh paint. Your artwork?"

"No! I would never!"

"I didn't think so."

I bent over to toss the cans in a nearby trash, but Dominic pulled my hand back. "Don't," he warned. "You'll leave fingerprints."

"Oh. Right." I stared at his hand holding my wrist and tingled with hot embarrassment. Jerking away, I said we'd better go.

Wait, your locker. It was Opal again.

I stopped. I thought, maybe I should listen this time.

"What?" said Dominic.

"We've got to check my locker."

Dominic just nodded and followed me down the hallway.

I quietly thanked Opal, because when I opened my locker, there were two spraypaint cans sitting inside.

"This Evan guy isn't messing around."

I nodded. Evan was clearly playing hardball.

*   *   *

When we finally stepped outside in the cool night air, I sucked in a deep breath then let it out slowly. I was safe—for now.

There was a fluttering of wings and Dominic's falcon landed on the protective leather band he usually wore on his arm. I regarded the sleek bird with new respect. "Did Dagger really tell you I needed help?"

"Not in words, but I understand his gestures. It's really not hard. When he dips his head like that, he's showing he's proud of himself."

"Yes, you're a smart guy," Dominic added to the bird.

"Very smart," I said gratefully. "Tell him thank you."

Dominic nodded, and tilted his head back and closed his eyes for a moment. No sounds were exchanged, but Dagger seemed somehow to understand. Maybe Dominic got mind-pictures like my visions, only his were from animals. I wanted to ask him about his own gift, but my heart was fluttering, and I wasn't sure what I should say.

We had reached Nona's front yard, I turned to Dominic, my fingers lingering on the latch. "I better go inside."

"Yeah." He nodded.

"It's late. I have—homework."

"And I have chores."

But he didn't leave and neither did I. He looked at me, as if waiting for something. I was waiting, too, although I had no idea for what. Silence stretched between us, long and awkward, until he shoved his hands in his pockets and started to walk away.

"Wait!" I shouted, startling us both.

He turned. "What?"

"I—I just wanted to say—" I faltered. "To say—you came through for me tonight, and I'll never forget it. Thank you."

Then I whirled around and ran into the house.

24

Nona had left a note on the door for me. "Poker at Grady's. Casserole in the oven. Your mother called again."

I was exhausted physically and emotionally. The last thing I needed was a talk with my mother. It wasn't like we ever talked anyway; we argued. So I crumpled the note and tossed it into the garbage.

Sunday I woke up with dark circles under my eyes and purple bruises on my knees. I didn't feel very good, and ended up spending the day in bed, talking on the phone and watching videos with Nona. She fussed over me and didn't even bring up the unpleasant topic of my mother's call. I couldn't shake my worries, but for one blissful day I felt a little better.

Unfortunately, Monday came too soon, and I knew staying home from school wouldn't make my problems go away. On the outside, everything appeared normal. I did regular stuff like help Nona make breakfast, listen to Penny-Love's latest gossip on the walk to school, and meet Josh at my locker with a cheerful smile. But inside I was a jumble of nerves, imagining I was poised on a guillotine, waiting for the ax to fall. The ax teetered a little when Josh asked me if I minded going on another double date with Evan. Yes, I minded! Was this more of Evan's idea of fun?

"What's the problem?" Josh asked, clearly disappointed when I refused to go anywhere with Evan. "Are you still mad at him because of Danielle?"

"It's more than that."

"What?"

I remembered Evan saying that the football team would give him an alibi, that any accusations against him would backfire on me. Who would Josh believe? A new girlfriend or his childhood best friend? I didn't want to put this question to the test—not without solid proof.

"He just isn't someone I can respect. Not the way I respect you," I added, curling my fingers in Josh's gentle hand. "And maybe I'm selfish, but when we go out, I want to be with you alone."

"Can't argue with that. But at least try to get along with Evan, for my sake."

I shrugged, which wasn't a yes or a no.

All through first period, I squirmed in my seat, constantly expecting an announcement over the loudspeaker about the graffiti. But it never came. So during break, I detoured by the supply room and discovered the walls were clean. When I leaned close, I just smell ammonia and paint. Had the janitor cleaned up without reporting the crime? Or was the principal planning more questions and locker searches? At least I was safe there. But would Evan find another way to shift suspicion to me?

I had to find out what was going on, and I knew just the person to ask. After telling Josh I was skipping lunch to work on the newspaper, I found Manny busy in the computer room, putting the finishing touches on this week's edition of the *Shout-Out.*

"Hey, Beany." He looked up from his papers. "Coming to save a drowning guy from a sea of work? The edition is running late."

"Maybe later." I pulled up a chair next to him. "Have you heard anything about more vandalism?"

He lowered his voice, "Nothing. What's up?"

"Too much." I told him everything—well almost. I didn't mention Dominic, letting Manny assume I escaped from the supply room on my own.

"Not Evan Marshall!" Manny exclaimed. "I can't believe

it! He's fantastic on the football field. Are you sure he's guilty?"

"That is so typically a male reaction." I put my hands on my hips and glared at him. "Just because someone is good at sports doesn't make him a saint. Evan thinks he's so smart, bragging about trying to frame me. He's guilty all right, and I've got the bruises on my knees to prove it."

"Okay, okay." Manny drummed his fingers on the desk. "I'm shocked, but I believe you. It'll make a great story. As soon as I have solid proof, I'll print it."

"Danielle knows and I know, isn't that enough?"

"Not if we want to convince Dunlap. Aside from being a big supporter of school sports, he's tight with Evan's parents. They play golf together."

"But Evan is guilty. He only dated Danielle to use her. And she fell for him so hard, she'd do anything he asked—even steal a test. But when things went bad, he had to go after the test himself, and he must have attacked the janitor to cover his tracks."

"The janitor wasn't hurt as badly as he let on," Manny said. "He's out of the hospital—and out of a job because stolen school supplies were found in his locker. The school board is embarrassed that an employee turned out to be a thief, and they're refusing to let me run the story."

"But that's censorship!"

"Tell me about it," he complained. "I'm thinking of going underground with a special edition or selling it to the local newspaper."

"So what about Evan? He admitted his guilt, but I don't have any proof. Isn't there anything we can do?"

"Unless you want to go on record as a witness." He looked squarely into my face. "You'd have to tell everything. About Danielle, Evan—and yourself."

I felt the color drain from my face. "And have another school turn against me? No one believing me, accusing me of being crazy? I can't go through that again."

"You won't have to, Beany." He smiled. "Some people think I'm shallow, and I don't mind because it's mostly true. But I won't write a story that hurts a friend. So the investigation ends now."

"Thanks—but it's so unfair." I sagged in defeat. "Evan gets away with vandalism, battery, and trying to frame me. He'll ace his bio test and probably score the winning touchdown at the next game and get a scholarship from some big-time college recruiter. He wins everything."

"Hmmm—maybe not everything." Manny tilted his head thoughtfully. "Isn't his bio teacher Blankenship?"

"I think so. Why?"

"Because Mr. B is a huge fan of my Mystic Manny column." Manny grinned. "Which gives me an idea."

"What?" I asked cautiously.

"It'll involve some changes to this week's *Sheridan Shout-Out* and the special talents of my two favorite psychics."

"I don't know about Thorn, but I'll help." Hope rose in me. "So when do we start?"

"Now."

*   *   *

Instead of Josh driving me home from school, Thorn, Manny, and I walked to a half-hidden, brick candy shop at the end of Maple Street called Trick and Treats. When I stepped through the door, crystal chimes jangled and delicious chocolate smells wafted on the air. I couldn't believe I'd lived in Sheridan Valley for months without discovering this yummy shop. The cheerful red-and-white-decorated room was lined with glass cabinets and displays of chocolates in all shapes and flavors. I'm sure I gained ten pounds just inhaling the sweet aroma.

The owner, a thirty-something woman dressed conservatively in beige slacks and a yellow blouse, click-clicked toward us on high heels, and greeted Thorn with a hug. "About time, Thorn. I had a feeling you might turn up, so I made a fresh batch of taffy nutballs."

"Thanks Velvet, but they'll have to wait." Thorn gestured to us. "These are my friends, Sabine and Manny. We're here for your specialty."

"I hope it's chocolate," I said, looking around.

A display with chocolate-marble-fudge shaped like tiny shoes caught my attention. Next to that was a glass case of caramel and chocolate-chip apples. I couldn't figure out what we were doing here, but I'd long held the motto: Never say no to chocolate.

"Most people come here for chocolate," Thorn explained. "But I prefer the special room."

"I only invite special customers back here," Velvet added a little mysteriously. Then she led us through a short hall and into a darkened room. Once the light was flipped on, my eyes nearly popped out. From sugar treats into New Age delights—crystals, oils, candles, stones, books, jewelry, and more.

"Does my grandmother know about this place?" I asked, running my fingers over a smooth amber stone and admiring a seashell-covered box.

"What's her name?" Velvet's lilting voice had a hint of an English accent. She seemed so proper and refined, like someone who would be more comfortable leading a PTA meeting or serving a formal tea.

"Nona Wintersong."

"Ah!" Velvet beamed. "Her favorite scent is lilac and she has a weakness for divinity cream puffs. So, you're the granddaughter she mentioned. You have her eyes, although yours are more emerald green than hazel."

I blushed a little, then turned to look at Manny when he cried out, "Gross!" as he sniffed a yellow candle. "What the heck is this stuff? It smells like vomit."

"Cake-batter scent," Velvet explained with amusement. "Perhaps you'd prefer bayberry or honeysuckle."

"Maybe later." He turned from the candle display. I walked with him over to a bookshelf.

"So what are we doing here?" I asked in a low voice.

"Shopping. This looks promising," he added, plucking a book titled *Mastering the Elements of Luck* off a shelf.

Across the room, Thorn was admiring a gold spiked chain similar to the silver one around her neck. On another counter were rows of peculiar jars, boxes, and packets. And a colorful rope of dried herbs draped across a window like a curtain.

"Did you get that info from Danielle?" Manny glanced at me as he flipped pages.

"Yeah, but it wasn't easy tracking her down. When I found out gym was her last class, I caught her before she left school. She told me the bio test is scheduled for this Friday, and Evan has a copy of it. Danielle said this test will probably be multiple choice, like the last one."

"All the easier to cheat."

"So how do we stop him?"

"Mr. B will switch the test. Evan may think he has all the answers—but they'll be the wrong answers."

"Blankenship won't be easy to convince," I said, bending over to sniff a bayberry candle. "He hasn't changed his hairstyle or bought any new clothes since 1978. I doubt he'll be inclined to write a new test."

"But he will because he's very superstitious," Manny explained. "He takes the day off every Friday the thirteenth and will walk a mile to avoid a black cat. We can't just blurt out that Evan plans to cheat without explaining how we know—which could get complicated. So we'll create an unlucky test."

I sighed and sank down onto a small cushioned bench. "He'll never believe that."

Manny sat beside me, setting the book on luck on his lap. "Don't doubt the persuasive powers of Mystic Manny. I convinced Pauline Shoemaker to go to the Winter Ball with me last year, even though she was dating someone else. And to raise money for a charity, instead of offering a free TV or concert tickets, I raffled off a scrawny abandoned kitten— and made over a thousand dollars. Persuading Mr. B will be easy."

"How do you make a test unlucky?"

"When Mr. B reads my Mystic Manny column tomorrow morning, he'll find a prediction warning a person in authority who carries a rabbit's foot and loves Zinc that Friday will bring misfortune unless precautions are taken."

"Zinc? Like the mineral?"

"Also the name of Mr. B's basset hound." Manny chuckled. "As a journalist and card-carrying snoop, I know all kinds of useful information about people. And I can calculate behavior. For instance, when Mr. B reads my column, he'll want to know what precautions to take against bad luck."

"So he'll come to you for advice?" I liked this crazy idea even though I had serious doubts it would work.

"Exactly. When he shows up, I'll offer him a good luck charm and warn him of papers in an unlucky order."

"That's too cryptic. Just him tell Evan plans to cheat."

"He's superstitious, not stupid. I can't accuse one of his students without strong evidence. But don't worry, I got it all figured out." Smiling confidently, Manny pointed in the book to a list of ingredients to ward off bad luck. "Mr. B will only be impressed if I give him an authentic good luck charm. So we'll need a pinch of crushed bone, stinkweed, and beetle extract. Combine them into a powder and pour it into a small cotton pouch."

In the strangest shopping trip of my life, we found everything except the beetle extract, but Velvet assured us that worm extract was a generic substitute. By the time we were finished, we had a lumpy, odd-smelling good-luck sachet.

Manny also bought the book on bad luck. "It's fascinating," he said, pointing to a page with a spooky picture of a skull and scrawny cat. "Did you know that sailors kept cats on their ships for luck and some of the superstitions about black cats go back to King Charles I?"

Only half-listening, I shrugged, my attention focused across the room where Thorn was whispering with Velvet. I thought Velvet was giving a phone number when I overheard her say "four" and "ten," but I could have been wrong. There was more whispering, then Thorn followed Velvet back into the candy room.

When Thorn reappeared minutes later, she was alone.

"What's up?" I asked her. "Where were you just now?"

Her purple-black lips curved in a mysterious smile. "With Velvet."

"Doing what?"

"Mixing up something for Blankenship."

"What?" Manny asked, giving her a puzzled look. "We only came for a good luck sachet."

"This is something extra." Thorn handed Manny a small object wrapped in shiny foil. "It's fragile, so hold it gently. And do NOT open it."

"What's inside?" Manny asked.

"A secret." She pretended to zip her lips.

"Give us a hint," I begged.

"Okay—a small one."

Manny and I leaned close to listen.

"It won't work unless you break it. Then if you want, you can eat it." Her kohl-shadowed eyes sparkled. "And it tastes delicious."

25

Lunch break the next day was torture. Josh talked me into joining his friends in the cafeteria, and I reluctantly agreed. Sitting across a table from Evan made each bite of my sandwich taste like cardboard.

Evan played me like a well-fed cat toying with a cornered mouse. He brought up the topic of double dating, then pretended to be hurt when I refused to go.

"That's too bad," he said sounding sincerely disappointed. "Have I done something to offend you?"

He actually looked me in the eye when he said this. I

would have given anything to be honest. But Josh was watching. "Of course not," I lied.

"Great! Let's plan another double date. You can even pick the movie."

"That's so generous of you," I said through clenched teeth.

"I'm just a nice guy," he said with a chuckle. Then he turned to Josh, bringing up shared memories that excluded me.

In a final cruel twist of the knife, he turned and asked me, dripping with concern, "So, do you think they'll ever find out who vandalized the school?"

I could only mumble, "I don't know."

So, Evan came off like a nice guy, and I sounded like a selfish jerk. It took extreme self-control not to fling my lunch in his face.

You won't always win, I wanted to shout at Evan. Not everyone is dazzled by your cocky grin and football finesse. When you push people too far, they push back and they push hard.

I crossed my fingers under the table and thought about Manny's plan. The *Shout-Out* was all over school, and Mystic Manny had students buzzing with curiosity.

*   *   *

By my last class, I was exploding with curiosity. "What's been going on?" I asked Manny. "Any news? Has he talked to you yet?"

"Shssh!" Manny put his finger to his lips, then led me over to the back of the room. "And no, Mr. B hasn't shown up."

"But he's had all day."

"You think he's going to discuss something this personal when anyone else is around? He'll wait till school ends. Be patient."

Why was everyone telling me to wait? Did I have "Impatient" tattooed on my forehead? Okay, so I wanted things to happen quickly. Like now.

After the final bell rang and only the teacher, Manny, and I were still in the computer lab, guess who showed up? Smoothing his garish polyester jacket, Mr. Blankenship cleared his throat nervously. Then he strode over to Manny and the two retreated to a quiet corner of the room.

I ducked behind a bulky computer terminal, close enough to hear Mr. B say, "… my dog Zinc. I knew the message was meant for me. Your last column was right on the mark with the prediction about green meaning money— I found a ten-dollar lottery ticket the next day. So, I can't ignore this. You'll help, won't you?"

"No prob," Manny said smoothly. "I was expecting you."

"Astonishing. You are truly a gifted young man."

"It's just what I do," he said humbly, and I almost gagged.

"What precautions do I need to take?"

"Take this charm," Manny offered. "It'll ward off bad luck."

"Unusual odor." Blankenship sniffed, puckering his face. "But why do I need this when I already have a rabbit's foot?"

"You can never have too much luck. And you'll need it … there's something … an image of a classroom …"

Manny draped his hand across his forehead and said melo-dramatically, "I see … a desk calendar shows a date … to-morrow … you're handing out papers … "

"I do that every day," Mr. B said with a dismissive shake of his head.

"But there's something different with these papers … disorder … danger."

"From what? A paper cut?"

"Do not joke." Manny gave a shudder, then met the teacher's gaze solemnly. "The sachet offers protection, but you'll also need to make changes."

"I don't understand."

"You don't?" Manny wiped sweat from his forehead. "Well … uh … maybe this will help." He held out Velvet's mysterious package.

I sat on the edge of my chair, watching eagerly as the teacher ripped open the foil wrapper.

"A fortune cookie?" Mr. B said with a puzzled frown. "How's a cookie supposed to prevent bad luck?"

"You got me—I mean, good question." Manny added, "Uh—all will be revealed when you open it."

The bio teacher snapped open the cookie in two even halves. A curled slip of paper fluttered into his lap. As Blankenship read the tiny message, his puzzled expression eased into understanding.

"Yes, yes. Now I see," he murmured, pocketing the paper and rising to leave.

Don't put it away! I wanted to yell. Read it out loud!

Manny asked curiously, "What did it say?"

"As if I need to tell you." Blankenship chuckled and slapped Manny lightly on the shoulder. "Thanks! Keep up the good work on your column, son, you've been a great help. And keep this—I don't eat sugar." He tossed the broken cookie to Manny and walked out of the classroom.

"What just happened?" I asked, jumping up from my hiding place.

"I'm not sure."

"Will he change the test?"

"We'll find out tomorrow." Manny sighed, then popped half of the cookie in his mouth and tossed the other half to me.

Thorn was right about one thing—her surprise was delicious.

*   *   *

"You can't avoid her forever," Nona lectured me that evening. We'd finished dinner and instead of Nona going to her office, she'd led me into the living room for "A Serious Talk." We faced each other across the couch like adversaries over a chessboard. I felt like a pawn cornered by a queen when she handed me the phone.

"This has gone on long enough," my grandmother said firmly. "Your mother has her faults, but she's my daughter, and I won't see her treated like this."

"I don't know what you're talking about."

"You haven't returned her calls."

"Guess I forgot."

"I'm the forgetful one around here," Nona said with a wry smile. "Not you."

"She hates me."

"That's not true, honey. Your mother loves you—it was just that your gift scared her. She feels threatened by the other side and would rather pretend it doesn't exist. She's not going to change, so try to accept her."

"She's the one who won't accept me."

"You need to talk out your differences."

"I have nothing to say to her."

"But she has something to say to you."

"What?" The phone felt cold in my hand.

"My intuitive skills are a bit rusty these days. Dial the number and find out."

"She probably wants me to stop talking to Amy and Ashley since I'm a bad influence."

Nona's arms came around me. "Give her a chance," she said softly.

With a heavy sigh, I dialed the familiar number.

The phone rang and rang, but no one answered. When the answering machine finally picked up, I slammed the receiver down.

"She's not home," I said with relief. "What a shame."

"You could have left a message."

"Oops. Forgot." I shrugged innocently. "I'll try again later."

Nona gave me a knowing look, but let it drop.

For now, I had a reprieve.

Stalemate.

*　　*　　*

Wednesday came and went without any drama. School, friends, homework. Normal stuff.

I managed to avoid any more encounters with Evan. Thorn was gone Wednesday and Thursday on a field trip to the Sacramento County Courthouse for her government class, so we couldn't ask her about the fortune cookie.

By Thursday afternoon, I had a nagging feeling that something was wrong. And I realized Danielle hadn't been at school for two days. During lunch break, I asked around and found out she was sick again. Sick, or avoiding Evan? I sympathized with her, but wondered how she could afford to miss so much school. Didn't she care about her grades? A prickle of unease settled in my gut as I remembered the image of a dragonfly dripping blood. If Danielle skipped another day, I'd personally go over to her house to make sure she was all right.

*　　*　　*

"What was the message in the fortune cookie?" I asked Thorn when I finally ran into her Friday during break.

"Didn't you read it?" she asked.

"No, but whatever it said impressed Mr. B."

"Good. When Velvet told me I could create my own

fortune cookie, how could I resist? So I went with a simple, short message."

"What?"

"Three words." She smiled. "'Change the test.'"

Nothing subtle about Thorn, I thought with admiration. She wore her drama outside, but inside she operated on plain old common sense. "Simple and to the point," I told her. "It might just work."

"It *will* work. Don't put out negative karma or it will come back to bite you in the butt. What you need is some positive reinforcement." Thorn reached up to take off one of her dangling purple fishhook earrings. "Here."

I eyed it suspiciously. "What's this for?"

"Good luck."

Then the bell rang and she was hurrying off. I looked down at the earring in my hand. I wouldn't put it on, of course. I only wore tasteful gold studs or hoops. Still, there was something wonderfully weird about the gaudy purple stones on the silver hook and feather coiled around the center. Thorn didn't care about fitting in, what anyone thought, and the only rules she followed were self-made. A little drama on the outside might be fun.

When I met Josh for lunch, he pointed to the fishhook earring swaying from my left ear. "What's that for? Is it Halloween already?"

"No—I'm just trying out something different."

"How come?" he asked, tilting his head as he studied me.

"Maybe I've only been pretending to be normal, but

deep down I have a wild, dangerous side. My secrets would shock and disturb you."

"Not a chance."

"Yeah. I guess you're right," I said, a bit disappointed.

"You're great the way you are." He playfully tapped my earring. "So don't change anything. But if you want to wear a hook, that's cool. I'll just have to take up fishing."

"You've already caught me."

"And I'm not letting you go."

Smiling, we hooked fingers and headed for my favorite lunch spot, away from the buildings, on a grassy area with a wide willow tree spreading out like an umbrella. I was relieved he hadn't wanted to go in the cafeteria where I'd have to face Evan again.

But we'd only been alone for a few minutes before Evan showed up.

"Josh!" he exclaimed, shoving between us. "I've been looking all over for you." His smooth exterior had definitely cracked.

"What's up?"

"Everything's ruined." Evan raked his fingers through his tousled dark hair. "You gotta help me."

Josh set down his apple and put a calming hand on his friend's shoulder. "What happened?"

"Blankenship won't let me play in the next game! Says I'm off the team! And a scout will be here for our next game! I can't miss out on my chance! I deserved an A, but I flunked!"

"Your bio test?" Josh guessed. "The one you said was so important?"

"Yeah." Evan nodded. "I knew all the answers and was the first one to hand in my paper. Then, before class is even over, here comes Blankenship with my test marked up in red. I don't get it—what went wrong?"

I bit into a chocolate chip cookie to keep from smiling. The chocolate was yummy, but payback was sweeter.

"That sucks, man." Josh shook his head sympathetically. "Maybe you can work things out with your teacher—take a make-up test. I'll help you study."

"Forget that, Josh! There's no time to study. The scout's only gonna be here once. It's the only game that matters. What the hell am I going to do now?"

Evan hung his head, looking so miserable that, if I hadn't hated his guts, I might have felt sorry for him. Evan may have gotten away with the vandalism, but he hadn't succeeded at framing me and now he was off his precious team.

I must have been smiling, because suddenly Evan whirled toward me with a pointed finger, "You!" he growled. "I don't know how, but you did this!"

I blinked innocently. "Me?"

"This is all your fault! You'd do anything to cause problems cause you're jealous that Josh and I are tight."

"How could I have anything to do with your flunking a test?"

"You must've told Blankenship."

"I don't know what you're talking about," I said calmly.

"Liar!" He jabbed his finger close to my face. "You're behind this!"

"Back off, man," Josh said, gently pushing Evan's hand down. "What are you talking about?"

"She's trouble. Conniving, back-stabbing, sneaky, little bi—"

"Watch it! I don't know what your problem is, but you're way out of line."

"Look at her! Can't you see? She's happy I'm ruined. She's got it in for me." Evan's eyes narrowed to slits. "You can't believe anything she says—she'd make up anything to turn you against me. She's even crazier than Danielle, and Danielle is one messed-up chick."

"That's enough." Josh hands tightened to fists. Evan looked shocked.

"Josh! You know me."

"Yeah, I know you," he said with a grimace. "Too well. I can overlook most of the stuff you pull, but you've got no right to attack Sabine."

"You're taking her side against me?"

"Appears so," Josh said coolly.

"What would your brother say?" Evan glared at Josh.

I could see Josh tense. They faced each other, tight-lipped and angry.

"Fine!" Evan snapped at Josh, breaking their stare down. Then he turned to me, "Watch your back, Sabine. This is not over." And he stormed off.

I may have won this round, but the war had only begun. And I'd made a dangerous enemy.

26

During my final period, I congratulated Manny. "It worked. Evan flunked and he's off the team until his grades improve—which could be a quite a while without Danielle doing his homework."

"Couldn't happen to a more deserving guy." Manny said. "Didn't I tell you my powers of persuasion were infallible?"

"Thorn's fortune cookie helped."

"All part of my grand scheme, which came off beautifully, even if I say so myself."

"And you will," I teased. "Over and over."

"Why deny brilliance? But you and Thorn helped, too. We make a great team, like Charlie's Angels. I'm Charlie and you girls are my 'angels.'"

"Thorn would knock that grin off your face if she heard you say that. And there's nothing angelic about me—except sometimes I see angels."

"Like now?" Manny whipped his head around, as if expecting a winged-being to pop up behind him.

"No." I shook my head. "But Opal says people who attract trouble usually have a lot of angels watching over them. So you must have at least a dozen."

He barked out a laugh so loud that everyone turned to look. But shameless Manny just bowed and waved to the class while I scooted low in my chair and hid behind the latest earth-shattering *Shout-Out* article I'd been proofing, "Teachers with Bad Breath—Is Mouthwash the Answer?"

After school, I stopped by my locker and felt a bit abandoned when no one was there to meet me. Josh had left early for a dentist appointment and Penny-Love was rah-rahing at cheer practice. I saw a lot of familiar faces as I started for home, but not anyone I wanted to hang out with, until I spotted a black-haired girl heading away from school, her single fishhook earring swinging with each step.

"Thorn!" I called, hurrying to catch up with her. "Wait up!"

She stopped, grinning when she saw me. "Hey, Sabine. I've been hoping to see you. I heard about Evan."

"News travels fast."

"Especially when it concerns the most popular jock at

school. Everyone's talking about poor, poor Evan," Thorn said, her eyes twinkling under glitter eye shadow. "Off the team and flunking bio."

"Such a tragedy," I replied in mock sympathy.

"And after he worked so hard to stay on the team," Thorn added. "Trashing the school, painting walls, copying a test, knocking out the janitor, and—"

"Trying to frame me," I finished.

"Which backfired on him."

"Even Josh knows he's got problems. He's too loyal just to give up on Evan, but he won't fall for Evan's lies anymore. And no more double dates."

"So let's celebrate." Thorn adjusted her backpack straps. "Want to go to Trick and Treats for something sinfully chocolate? Anything you want—my treat."

"Oooh, sounds great!" My mouth watered, until I remembered that I'd promised Nona I'd come directly home today. "But I can't. Nona needs help with spring cleaning."

"Spring cleaning in the fall?"

"Nona doesn't follow normal rules. And she's done so much for me, I don't mind cleaning out the pantry and defrosting the freezer."

"Some celebration," Thorn grumbled. "Work, work, and more work."

"But there are perks of the job—like ice cream."

She brightened. "Ice cream?"

"A half-finished carton of Heavenly Hash may melt during the defrosting if someone doesn't eat it first."

"Say no more. I'm always willing to help a friend." Then Thorn gave me a deep look. "But are you sure—sure you don't mind being seen with me?"

"Why would I?" I tried not to think of Penny-Love's reaction to my hanging out with Thorn.

"Your preppy cheerleading girlfriends won't like it." Thorn wiggled the silver ring in her left eyebrow.

"You think that matters to me?"

"Well … doesn't it?"

"Maybe it did a little at first, but not now." I jiggled my fishhook earring. "Being a little different is cool."

"So, does that mean you'll let me dye your hair blood red and spike it?" She arched an eyebrow at me.

"Not that different." I punched her playfully, then we fell in step and talked all the way home.

At the entrance to our driveway, we stopped a moment while I checked the mailbox. Then I glanced at Thorn, wondering what she'd think of my home. It had taken me a week to work up the courage to invite Penny-Love over, and at first, she was put off by the dirt, weeds, and livestock smells. But she didn't complain anymore and got along great with Nona, always eager to hear matchmaking stories.

As Thorn and I walked down the driveway, her eyes widened at the farmhouse I now called home.

"I know it's rundown," I said before she had a chance to criticize. "It's older than air and needs a paint job, but that's so expensive, and Nona does plan to fix those window frames and the broken porch step."

"It's—It's … " Thorn shook her head. "Fabulous!"

"Really?"

"You're lucky to live in the country, instead of in a neighborhood where neighbors are close enough to hear you flush the toilet. Your animals are cool, too. Is that floppy-eared animal a goat?"

"Yeah. A Nubian."

Thorn spread out her arms expressively. "It's so roomy here. You should see the tiny box I live in—only three bed-rooms and I have five siblings. But you have all this space for only two people!"

"Actually three." I pointed to the barn where I could see Dominic lifting an ax and splitting wood.

"Who's that? Your brother?"

"No!" Heat rose in my cheeks. "We're not related—I barely know him. He's just Dominic. He helps with the chores."

"So he lives here?"

"Not in the house, the barn apartment."

"Cool. He looks about our age, but I haven't seen him at school."

"He could be a drop-out or have graduated early, for all I know. I've asked my grandmother, but she won't tell me any personal stuff about him." I shook my head. "Don't bother trying to talk to him. He's complicated—doesn't like people much. He's just—different." I changed the subject. "Anyway, you'll love my grandmother. Come on inside."

"Lead the way."

I pushed open the front gate and a streak of white zoomed by my legs, rubbing against my ankles. Picking up Lillybelle, I cuddled her silky body in my arms.

"What fabulous mismatched eyes. She's beautiful!" Thorn scratched Lillybelle by the ears and received an appreciative purr. "I wanted a cat, but my sister Meg is allergic. So we have fish."

"Lillybelle loves fish," I said teasingly.

"Well, she isn't invited over to my house. But you can come anytime."

"Is your family into the Goth look, too?"

"Not even!" She almost doubled over with laughter. "They're so Brady Bunch, I want to puke most of the time. They can't figure out what to make of me—and that's the way I like it."

Lillybelle squirmed in my arms and bounded toward the pasture as I stepped up on the porch. Opening the front door, I called out for Nona. She didn't answer and wasn't in the living room or her office. When I checked the kitchen, I found the freezer door open and packaged food stacked on the counters.

"Melted ice cream," Thorn said, picking up a soggy, dripping container that had once been Heavenly Hash. She licked her fingers. "But it still tastes yummy."

"I wonder why Nona started cleaning without me?"

"She must have got interrupted. It happens all the time at my place."

"Her car is here," I said with a peek out the front window. "So she has to be around somewhere."

We left the kitchen and went through the rest of the house. I was starting to get worried, when I opened her bedroom door and found her sleeping.

"My father makes little snoring sounds like that, too," Thorn whispered. "She looks so peaceful."

"How can she just go to sleep with food melting in the kitchen?" I shut the door quietly.

"She must be really tired."

"Nona has been working late hours," I admitted. "I'll let her sleep and finish up in the kitchen."

Thorn jumped right in and started cleaning with me. Most of the food was still frozen—except for the ice cream and a soggy bag that used to be ice cubes. As I stacked food back into the freezer, my fingers stung with icy cold. By the time I was done, my hands were almsot completely numb.

Running hot water over my chilled fingers helped a little. My hands warmed, tingling back to life. But the rest of me suddenly wasn't feeling so well. My head throbbed and my vision blurred. I stared down at the sink, mesmerized by the water pouring over my fingers. As I watched, the water darkened in color, from clear to blood red. Spilling on silverware and plates, swirling down the drain, flowing over my skin.

With a shriek, I stared down in horror at my hands. Was it really blood? Or was I going crazy? My left wrist throbbed, its color changing, too, as a dark shape with wings appeared etched in my flesh.

A dragonfly tattoo.

"NO!" I rubbed at the image. "Go away!"

Thorn tossed down a rag she'd been using to wipe the counter and hurried over to me. "What's wrong?"

"The water! My wrist!" I cried, trembling. "It's on me!"

"What? Are you hurt?"

"Look!" I stuck my arm out toward her. "Don't you see it?"

"See what?" She shook her head, and when I looked back down, my hand had returned to normal. The blood and the dragonfly were gone.

"Talk to me, Sabine. Are you sick?"

I gulped a deep breath. "It's not me ... it's her."

"Who?"

"Danielle." Fear thumped with my rapid heartbeats. "Either I'm losing my mind or I just had a vision—a warning. Danielle's in trouble."

"Go with your gut." Thorn shut off the water faucet, then turned back to me. "Do you know her phone number?"

"Yeah," I said, relieved Thorn understood and didn't ask any unnecessary questions. Seconds later, I was dialing the number.

But it was busy.

"Why doesn't she have call waiting?" I complained, slamming the receiver down.

"Want to keep trying?" Thorn asked.

"I don't think there's time. I don't know what's going on, just that I'm supposed to help her."

"Then we'll help her," Thorn said. "Together."

I ran to the hook where Nona normally left her car keys, but they weren't there. I thought about Nona's recent tendency to hide things from herself, and I wasn't sure if there was any point in looking for them. I went into her room and whispered softly, "Nona, I need to use your car. Do you know where you left your keys?"

"Helene? Is that you? What do you need?" She rolled over and seemed to fall back to sleep. Nona was obviously exhausted; Helene was my mother's name. Finding the keys could take time we didn't have. We needed to get going.

Walking to Danielle's house wouldn't be fast enough, so I went to the shed where I kept my bicycle. Nona had a bike, too, and I offered it to Thorn. We started to kick off, when I heard a motor and saw an approaching cloud of dust. A white Dodge truck roared to a stop in front of us.

Dominic rolled down the window. "Need a ride?"

I was tempted to ask if Dagger had been spying on me again, but I was so grateful for the offer that I just nodded. "Thanks. Driving will be faster."

Thorn was eyeing Dominic. Did she sense that he was different like us? Or was she interested in him the way Penny-Love had been? There wasn't time for polite introductions, so I skipped that part and gave Dominic directions to Danielle's house.

When the truck slowed to a stop five minutes later, my

seatbelt was already off and I flew up a stone walkway to the door. I pressed the bell, over and over, until a tall man I recognized as Danielle's father showed up.

Mr. Crother frowned at me. "One push of the bell would suffice."

"Where's Danielle?"

"Upstairs in her room."

"I have to see her now," I said, aware that Thorn had come up beside me. "I tried to call, but the line was busy."

"I was on the computer." He looked at us for a moment. "Go on up, but Danielle is probably sleeping. I haven't seen her in hours."

"Hours?" I repeated uneasily. Then I bolted past him, up the stairs, Thorn's footsteps pounding behind mine. I tried two doors, one was a linen closet and the other a bathroom, before I stepped into a feminine, pink-and-white room decorated with a shelf of dolls from other countries and a canopy bed covered with stuffed toys and a patchwork quilt.

But there was no Danielle.

"So where's your friend?" Thorn asked.

"Not here." I frowned. "Something's terribly wrong."

Mr. Crother appeared in the doorway and looked around with a puzzled expression. "That's odd. I was sure Danielle was up here. She hasn't been well and has been sleeping a lot."

Beyond the room's cheerful pink decor, a gray aura of sadness was overwhelming. "So where is she?"

Mr. Crother shrugged. "Maybe with her boyfriend."

"They broke up," I told him.

"They did? But she never said anything."

"Haven't you noticed how unhappy she's been?" I asked.

"Well she hasn't felt well. I thought it was a mild flu."

"I'm afraid it's more than that." I frowned. "Do you have any idea how long she's been gone?"

"She didn't tell me she was leaving." He rubbed his chin anxiously. "This isn't like her. She's always very dependable and let's us know where she's going. Danielle is such a good girl."

"What's that on her pillow?" Thorn stepped into the room and picked up a paper. "An envelope—addressed to you." She handed it to Mr. Crother.

"See, I told you my girl is reliable. She just didn't want to interrupt my work, so she left a note. She's always doing thoughtful things like that."

He ripped into the envelope and withdrew a single sheet of paper. As he read, his face drained of color and he sagged against the bed.

"What is it?" Thorn and I asked, coming to his side.

"She can't! She wouldn't—" he choked on his words.

"Is it from Danielle?"

He nodded weakly and held out the letter. He looked as if he'd aged twenty years in seconds and seemed con-fused. "Read it. Tell me what you think."

I held the letter so Thorn could see to, then read the

short scrawled message: "I can't go on without him. Not anymore. Sorry I let everyone down... Danielle."

I gasped. "Ohmygod!"

"This sounds like a sui—!" Thorn stopped when she saw the stricken look on Mr. Crother's face. He grabbed the letter back and clutched it to his chest, clearly in shock.

My visions had nothing to do with the vandalism, I realized. I'd been so focused on denying my gift and playing Nancy Drew that I hadn't realized the danger for Danielle wasn't from Evan—but from herself. And while getting back at Evan felt good, it was only a small victory. Danielle was more important.

Mr. Crother seemed to recover, jumping up and grabbing a phone. He forget about us as he barked out orders to the police. I was glad he was taking action, but would the police find her soon enough? An hourglass flashed in my head, not filled with sand, but with life minutes ticking away.

Danielle could be anywhere—miles from here or hiding nearby. I had no idea how to find her. "Opal," I thought desperately. "Interfere just this once, I'm begging you. I can't do this alone."

I thought I heard a soft reply, *You're not alone.*

"So tell me where Danielle is," I begged. Then I waited, listening for an answer. Only none came, and my frustration boiled to anger.

"I didn't ask for any of this!" I silently raged. "I can't go through another tragedy, always wondering if I could have prevented it. You say I'm not alone, yet I'm standing here with no answers and no one to help me."

There was a tap on my shoulder and my fishhook earring slapped my neck as I turned to Thorn. "Are you okay?" she asked.

I started to shake my head, then looked at Thorn—really looked—and realized that Opal was right. I wasn't alone.

"Thorn!" I exclaimed. "You can find anything, right?"

"Most of the time. But what—"

"What about people?" I interrupted, grasping her hands. "Can you find Danielle?"

27

Thorn sorted through the stuffed animals on Danielle's bed before picking up a pink bunny and hugging it, her eyes closed tight with concentration.

"I've never done this before," she murmured. "Not with a person."

"It can't be that different than finding a fencing grip or lost keys."

"Oh, it's different." She frowned and drifted off somewhere with her mind. Long seconds had gone by before she finally spoke. "It's faint—a sense of distance."

"How far?"

"More than a mile, but I don't know how much more. It's not working!" She threw the pink bunny down. "I'm trying, really, but it isn't just a game, it's real life…or death. I'm not sure she's—she's still—"

"Don't even think that! You're the one who says to be positive, so follow your own advice. Try harder—you can do it."

"Maybe if I hold something she's touched recently." She picked up the envelope Danielle's father had discarded, and ran her fingers over the scrawled writing on the front.

"Well?" I asked impatiently.

"This is better. She's somewhere familiar to her, a place that used to make her feel happy…now there's only despair."

"Evan's house?" I guessed.

"Could be—but it doesn't feel like a house. A large open place, grassy with benches." She rubbed her forehead, wincing as if feeling pain.

"A park?"

"No, that doesn't feel right. There's some kind of school connection."

"The school quad? It's grassy and there are benches. But I doubt she'd go there."

"Are you sure?"

I bit my lip. How could I be sure of anything? If anyone had told me that Danielle was suicidal, I wouldn't have believed that either. I'd gotten warnings, saw the bloody dragonfly. I should have known, been a better friend, tried to help her.

You are helping, Opal assured. *Open up your mind and trust yourself.*

And just like that, I got it. A lightning flash burst in my head, and I saw rows of tiered benches and a field of rough grass. A small shape lay crumpled on the dirt.

"Not benches—bleachers!" I jumped excitedly. "I know where Danielle is!"

"You do?" Thorn asked.

"At the school. You were right about that." I said grimly. "We have to get there before it's too late—if it isn't already!"

Night had fallen, and when we hurried back to Dominic's truck, he had the lights on and the motor running. After a quick explanation, Thorn and I hopped inside and Dominic revved the engine. We sped toward the school. No one complained when Dominic pushed us past the legal limit.

I hoped that Dominic had an army of angels guiding him because he didn't stop, only paused for a quick look, before speeding through two stop signs. Tires screeched as Dominic pulled into the school, not turning for the student parking lot, but roaring to the front lot reserved for teachers and buses.

"The football field!" I breathed out. "She's there—by the bleachers, where she watched Evan."

Thorn told us to go after her, while she'd get help. Dominic and I didn't slow down, racing around buildings, breathing hard, feet pounding on pavement. We headed for the bleachers—and that's where we found her.

Lying on the dirt near the bleachers, still and fragile, blood pooling around her outstretched arm. She didn't move and her face was deathly pale.

"Ohmygod!" I gasped hoarsely. "We're too late!"

Dominic knelt beside her and felt for a pulse.

"Is she—?" I asked in a trembling voice.

"Not yet, but she's in bad shape."

I let out a huge, relieved breath. "Hold on, Danielle," I murmured. "You're going to be okay."

There was no response.

Dominic ripped off the strip of leather he wore on his arm as a perch for his falcon. He wrapped it tightly around Danielle's wrist, slowing the flow of blood.

There was sudden blinding light, and for a moment I thought angels were coming for Danielle, until I realized someone had switched on the field lights. Turning, I saw Thorn leading a young, nervous janitor over to us.

Within minutes, there was a dizzy rush of voices, sirens, and uniforms. Danielle got first aid and was then whisked away in an ambulance. I went with her, since she seemed so alone, in need of a friend. Thorn and Dominic said they'd meet us at the hospital after they answered questions from the police.

My first ride in an ambulance and I was only aware of Danielle, who was unresponsive as paramedics worked over her. There was nothing to do but watch and pray.

At the hospital, I was directed to a waiting room, where I sat numbly in a hard plastic chair. Nearby, a young mother bit her lip while she clung to a sleeping baby and an elderly man stared blankly at a television fixed high on the wall.

And I waited.

As minutes ticked slowly by on a wall clock, I thought about Danielle and how precious life was—how fragile, too. She'd been on a dangerous course for a long time, only no one had noticed. She'd been what everyone expected: perfect daughter, top student, loyal girlfriend. Yet it wasn't enough, and somewhere along the way she lost herself. She'd kept her secrets so well, it would have been too late to save her—if it hadn't been for my visions.

She just has to make it, I thought, still staring at the clock. I crossed my right leg, then my left. I picked up a magazine, then set it aside without looking at it. I shifted to another chair with a better view of the door. What was happening?

The door burst open, and Danielle's father entered with a slender, black-haired woman who was obviously Danielle's mother. The woman sank on the couch beside the couple with the baby, while Danielle's father spotted me and came over.

"Thank you," Mr. Crother told me.

"For what?"

"They said you found her. She's holding on but the doctor said if she'd lost any more blood..." His voice cracked. "That we would—would have lost our daughter."

"I'm glad she's okay."

"You saved her life," he said. "I—I just felt so useless when I read that letter. Didn't have any idea where to look. But you found her. How did you know?"

"My friends helped. But we didn't really know either—it was a lucky guess."

"Or an answer to our prayers," he said, giving my hand a tight squeeze.

I knew in that moment that I could tell him the truth about how I really found Danielle. He wouldn't call me a freak or crazy. He would believe me.

A burden inside me lifted on wings and fluttered away. Foretelling bad things didn't mean I'd caused them to happen—and this time I'd saved a life.

28

After a while, Dominic and Thorn picked me up from the hospital. We dropped Thorn off at a single-story home, where toys littered a small patch of front lawn, and then Dominic and I headed back home. When he stepped out of his truck, there was a screech overhead and his falcon fluttered down to greet him.

"Dagger wants a snack," Dominic said with a tired smile. "I'll be in the barn if you need anything."

I looked into his eyes, sending him a silent message of thanks. He nodded, which seemed enough. For now.

Feeling strangely happy, I hurried to the house. Nona must have been watching for me because she rushed out, almost knocking Lillybelle off her favorite perch on a porch rail. "Oh, honey! How is your friend?"

"Alive."

"Thank the heavens."

"She's going to make it, but it'll take time before she's well enough to go back to school," I added.

"Poor child. Her troubles must run deep."

"No troubles are worth killing yourself over. Why would she do something that dumb? Just because her boyfriend dumped her?"

"I'm sure it's more than that. I've seen clients desperate to fill emptiness by clinging to someone else."

"Like Evan," I said with a frown.

"Your friend needs to love herself. With supportive people around, she'll be all right."

"I hope so."

Nona gave me another hug. "I'm proud of you, honey."

"I didn't do anything special."

"You followed your heart and used your gift to save that girl."

"My gift?" I did a double take. "But you said I'd outgrown it."

"For a while, I thought you had. You put on a good show and nearly convinced me. You're the one who denied your ability."

"Then you believe me?"

"I never really stopped, but I knew it was your choice whether you followed your talents. And I'm delighted you made the right decision."

"Are you sure it's the right one?" I asked. "I hear voices, see things that other people can't, and get warnings that scare me. What kind of gift is that?"

"A precious one. Your ability isn't for you—it's for the world." She looked deep into my eyes and added, "My darling Sabine—*you* are the gift."

* * *

That night, a sharp noise jerked me out of a dream where my mother had grown into a giant and was chasing me around the barn, trying to stomp me with spiked, truck-sized boots.

Bolting up in my bed, I looked around expecting Mom to burst out from the shadows. I stared around my familiar room and drew comfort from the soft yellow glow of my smiley-faced nightlight. I didn't need to check Nona's dream interpretation book to understand my nightmare. Right before I'd gone to bed, Nona had delivered the bad news. My mother had called again, only instead of leaving a new message for me to ignore, she was coming to see me next week.

I'd rather be stomped by giant, spiked shoes.

But the dream wasn't what had awakened me, I realized when I heard a sharp bang and cry from downstairs.

Putting on a robe, I hurried to Nona's office and found the door wide open, a triangle of light slicing into the hall.

My grandmother sat on the floor among a pile of papers with a terrified look on her face.

"I—I can't find it," she whispered, tears streaming down her cheeks.

"Find what?" I sat beside her and gently took her hand.

"That's the problem—I don't know."

"What's going on? Nona, you're scaring me."

"I'm scaring me, too." She gave a brittle laugh and wiped her cheek. "I've been putting this off—telling you—but I can't anymore."

"I don't understand."

"You will soon." Papers scattered as she stood. "Follow me."

There was something desperate and determined in her voice that stopped me from asking any more questions. Silently, I walked behind her as she stepped outside, passed the chicken pen, and entered the barn. She snapped on a light, then called upstairs to Dominic.

"Why are we here?" I whispered anxiously. "We'll wake up Dominic."

"That's the idea."

A door from the loft creaked open and Dominic's tousled head peaked out. I could only see the top of his bare shoulders and a glimpse of dark shorts.

He only needed one look at Nona's grim expression; then, he turned around and returned a moment later fully clothed. He opened the door in invitation, and Nona led me upstairs toward his apartment.

Dominic pulled up two chairs and gestured for us to sit, while he faced us on the edge of his rumpled bed. It felt odd to sit so close to him, and I scooted my chair back a few inches.

Nona clutched at the fabric of her terry-cloth robe and biting her lips. "Dominic, it happened again ... only worse."

"Are you okay?"

"That isn't the issue right now. I have to be honest with both of you. What I'm going to tell you won't be easy," she said in a quavering voice.

"You don't have to say anything," Dominic said, his tone protective.

"I want to—while I still can."

I looked at Nona. "Does this have to do with whatever you lost tonight?"

"That's part of it. You've probably noticed that's happened a lot, my forgetting or losing things. At first it was small episodes, missing keys or not calling back a client. Then tonight I panicked and started tearing apart my office."

"What did you lose?" I asked.

"It's not what I lost, but what I'm losing." She lifted her shoulders and gave Dominic a steady, determined look. "Get the box."

"But you told me never to—"

"Just get it for me," she said firmly. "Please."

Dominic's jaw tightened stubbornly, but he didn't argue. He rose and crossed the room, stopping before a wall portrait of a forest scene. Dominic lifted the picture and set it down, then pressed one hand against the wall where I saw the faint square outline of a hidden cupboard.

"Here," Dominic said a bit angrily, withdrawing an antique silver box and handing it to Nona. "I hope you're doing the right thing."

"What is it—Pandora's box?" I half-joked.

But no one laughed, and I sensed that my joke held a deep truth.

Nona didn't open the box, instead reaching for my hand. "Sabine, there's something I've been keeping from you." I started to interrupt, but she put her hand up. "Let me say this before I lose my nerve. You see, I—I'm not well. It's a genetic affliction. One that goes back nearly three hundred years."

"Nona!" I choked out. "You're not—"

"No, it isn't fatal, but it might as well be," she said bitterly. "I watched my great-aunt Letitia suffer from it, and by the time I learned there was a cure, she was beyond help."

"So there's a cure?" I asked hopefully.

"Yes. But—" Her voice quavered. "But it was lost during a dark period in our family history. One of our ancestors created a remedy, then had to hide it when she was accused of being a witch. Directions to the hiding place were divided between her four daughters, including a many-times great-grandmother of mine."

"Is that what's in the box?"

"No. But it's a clue—and Dominic has been helping me figure it out."

"Why him and not me?" I asked, fighting the hurt.

"You know that answer," she replied with a pointed look. And I sagged in my chair, blaming myself for denying my gift for so long. Wasted time when I could have been helping Nona.

"Tonight I didn't even remember going into my office," she went on in a frightened voice. "It's happening more and more, moments of my day becoming black holes. Moments, minutes, lost memories. Soon I may even forget you."

I swallowed back tears, fighting to be brave for my grandmother, although my heart was breaking. I'd never been happier than these months living with her. I couldn't lose that—lose her.

"What can I do to help?" I asked.

"Work with Dominic to find the remedy."

"Him?" I shot a resentful glance at Dominic, then swallowed my pride and gave a slow nod. "Okay. How do I start?"

"With this."

She lifted the ornate silver box and placed it gently in my arms.

"Everything you need is inside. Go ahead—open it."

The End

Dominic's Volcano

He'd carefully planned the escape.

Only when he heard the sputter and backfire of his uncle's truck fade to a distant rumble did Dominic push off the rough blanket and spring from his cot. Adrenaline pumping, he opened the door of the mud room; the airless hole which doubled as his bedroom reeked of diesel from the jackets hanging like dead things on the wall. He hated the room almost as much as he hated his uncle.

Almost.

The door thudded behind him as he left for the last time.

His uncle had made no pretense about his hate for Dominic, resenting that the only inheritance he'd gained from the untimely death of his younger sister was a rough-edged teen. Uncle Jim only tolerated his orphaned nephew for the monthly government checks.

Although Dominic knew enough not to expect a loving home, he hadn't been prepared for his uncle's drinking, bad temper, and cruel hand. But bitter lessons quickly taught him how to hide on Saturday nights and never to argue when his uncle's whip was within reach.

His only solace was Volcano, his uncle's hunting dog. Volcano was about eight years old, some kind of shepherd-lab mix, and starved for attention. Together they shivered outside on bitter nights, hiding from drunken anger and the whip. It was during these trembling times that an odd thing happened. Boy and dog communicated—not in words but in mental picture messages. A warm blanket, a bowl of food, a scratch behind the ears—Dominic always knew what Volcano needed, and the dog understood him, too.

But last night Uncle Jim's cruelty ignited the beginning of the end.

Sounds of yelping and swishing leather bled in the night. Dominic, hiding high in a tree, heard the cruel attack but was unable to do anything but cringe and burn with helpless rage. He lacked fighting strength—his painful wounds from recent beatings left him too weak to do more than huddle in the dark. When the brutal sounds died away and the house door slammed, Dominic made his way back to Volcano, cradling the whimpering dog and vowing "never again."

All that night he cradled his only friend, crooning words of comfort, unable to sleep as he stared up at the ceiling, planning.

Escape was the only way out.

He'd take Volcano far away, to someplace without anger and whips—if such a place existed. His mother had believed in the good in people, and made excuses for her older brother even after he attacked their father and stole money before leaving home. As she breathed her last breath, she'd still believed in impossible things like heaven, forgiveness, and love.

Now hate was the only reality for Dominic; it was the driving force that pushed him. If he stayed any longer, his simmering violence would erupt and things might happen that would make him no better than his uncle.

"Come on, boy," he whispered to Volcano as he gently lifted off the spiked collar and released the dog. Blood-slashed stripes lay across the dog's back, and Dominic's anger seethed. He found a cloth, dampened it, and gently rubbed Volcano's silky brown fur, brushing away dried blood and untangling mats.

Holding tight to his self-control, Dominic watched the soothing images Volcano sent to him, of wagging tails and a soft bed in a safe house. Volcano held no hate; there was only hope shining from his liquid dark eyes.

Dominic had already decided that the only way to protect Volcano was to find him a new home: a house with a big yard, kids, and a soft doggy bed where he could safely sleep at night. So he packed a small knapsack of clothes and pictures of his lost life, also taking along a black pen and square of cardboard.

They trudged miles to the nearest town, through a forest of uneven ground and then down a long winding highway. As morning heated to humid afternoon, Volcano whined and sent a mind image of a big bowl of water.

"Sorry, boy," Dominic said in a hoarse, dry-mouth voice. "But soon."

River Crest was too small to be considered a city, with its one church, two bars, post office, and small store. The wooden bench in front of the store provided rest and shade. Dominic longed to buy water for Volcano and a Coke for himself, but he had no money. There was nothing to do but wait, and cling to a remote hope that his mother's belief in the deep-down goodness of people was true.

On the cardboard, he wrote a simple message: Free dog to good home.

Then they both waited; the dog thumped his tail hopefully whenever little kids walked by, but Dominic kept his face averted, emotionless. He didn't care if he was sweaty and dirty in hard-worn clothes. He didn't care about the hunger that gnawed at his gut. He only cared about the dog, faithful and trusting and deserving of a better life.

But there didn't seem to be a morsel of goodness from people who passed by—only curiosity and suspicion. When a little girl asked if she could pet the dog, her mother slapped her hand and hustled her inside the store.

After several long, hot hours, the store owner strode out, his thinning head dripping with sweat and his mustache drooping in a perpetual scowl. "Customers have been complaining," he told Dominic with no heart in his words. "You and your mutt will have to move on."

His mother was wrong about there being some good in everyone, Dominic thought.

Holding himself proud, he stood to leave, sending comforting thoughts to Volcano.

"Wait!" a woman's voice rang out. "Young man, please come here."

Dominic turned. He noticed how the store owner tensed, as if the woman—with her graying blond hair upswept under a wide-brimmed straw hat and her long flowered skirt sweeping dust out of her way—possessed some kind of power. There was something commanding in the lift of her chin, the soft and wise wrinkles around her eyes, and the forceful arch of her brows. And Dominic stopped.

Instead of speaking to Dominic, the woman waved a scolding finger at the store owner. "Ron, have you offered this weary young man and his dog something to drink?"

"What?" He wiped his damp forehead, shaking his head. "No, ma'am."

She frowned. "Well, why in heaven not? I can't imagine a church-going man like you allowing an animal and a boy to suffer on such a hot day."

Sweat dripped from the store owner's brow as he looked uneasily at Dominic, then back to the woman. "I have a business to run, ma'am."

"Which includes good customer relations." She swiveled back to Dominic. "Young man, what do you like to drink?"

Dominic hesitated, afraid this was a trick question. He wasn't sure what was going on and was poised to run if things went bad.

"Aren't you thirsty?" the woman insisted.

"Don't matter about me." Dominic kept his gaze low. "But my dog could use water."

"Go on, Ron, you heard the boy. And why not bring out two Cokes while you're at it? If that's a problem for you, add them to my bill."

"It's not a problem." With a frown, the store owner headed back inside.

The woman bent over to read Dominic's sign. "So you're selling this fine dog?"

"Not selling." He shook his head. "I don't own him."

"So who does?"

"Volcano owns himself."

"Wise answer," she said, with a smile that softened her wrinkles. "You have an intriguing aura, young man. And it's clear you have a real bond with your dog. So why aren't you keeping him?"

"My uncle is allergic to dogs."

"What a shame. This must be hard on you."

"I'll be fine. But Volcano deserves kids to play with and a big yard for running. He needs a good home."

"Looks like you do, too."

Dominic didn't answer, cautious.

"You live around here?" she asked.

"No." This would be true enough, soon.

The store owner came out, his scowl deepening as he handed the woman two Cokes and set out a bowl of water for the dog. Abruptly, he strode back into the store.

"Ron isn't usually so gracious," the woman said with a laugh.

Dominic cracked a small smile, relaxing for the first time all day.

"So would your dog like to go home with me?"

"Do you have a big yard?"

"Is ten acres big enough?"

Dominic nodded, knowing his mother would have liked this unusual woman with her wide hat and bossy attitude. Dominic sent a message to Volcano, showing a doggy bed and the woman feeding him meaty bones. But Volcano whined, sending back a vision of himself beside Dominic.

"He'd doesn't care about bones or a dog bed," the woman said. "He'd rather stay with you."

Dominic jumped back, staring suspiciously. "How do you know that?"

"Sometimes I just know things."

"How?"

"The same way you do."

"I don't know what you're talking about."

"You will when we meet again. Someday," she said with a look that reached deep inside him. "But until then all I can do is take care of what you need now. So I will be honored to give your dog a good home."

"You will?" Suspicion shifted to something close to happiness.

"I live on a farm where there's plenty of room for your dog. My husband is an artist and he recently lost his dog of eighteen years. Volcano will be great company for him, and will have the run of our fields, then come inside every night and sleep in his own dog bed. Also, my granddaughter Sabine visits often and is a big animal lover."

Dominic didn't know what to say; somehow this strange woman had said it all.

Then came the hardest part—letting go of his only friend. He wished he could go, too, but Volcano would be safer starting over completely, with no ties to his former life. And Volcano seemed to understand this. After lapping up every drop of water, he calmly walked over to the woman and sat under the shade of her wide hat.

The huge weight of worry lifted from Dominic.

Volcano would be safe.

"Contact me if you need anything," she said, handing him a small card.

He nodded, thanking her again and walking away before he lost the courage to leave. Only after he was a mile away, too far to run back, did he stop to read the business card. First he memorized the address, then slowly he read the woman's name:

~ *Nona Wintersong* ~
Psychic Medium

*   *   *

Dominic trudged down a seemingly endless highway, his thumb out. He hoped a trucker would pick him up so he could travel far away to another state. But when nightfall came, his thumb was still out and a hole was worn through his right boot. Shivering with cold, he ached with a hunger so deep it stole his strength. Wearily, he turned from pavement and rushing vehicles toward the woods.

When Dominic was little, he and his mother lived high on a wooded hill, his playground nature's wild forests. His mother trusted him to roam outside, respecting his unusual rapport with animals: squirrels, raccoons, and even the shyest deer would nuzzle up to him. The woods had sheltered him the way his uncle should have.

Once again he found refuge in nature. His night vision had always been unusually sharp, and with the help of a faint moon and the stars shining on the animal trails, he found bushes with ripe berries and a hollowed grassy spot perfect for sleeping. A doe and her fawn rested nearby, and although he didn't know how to share mind images with them like he could with Volcano, their closeness calmed him.

When morning brightened, he found a stream and

drank cool water. Splashing his face, he felt more alive than ever, now that he was no longer chained to an uncle who despised him. He could live here, if he chose. Maybe he would … but somehow that felt wrong, as if he had a different destiny.

He spent hours by the river trying to catch fish, but his rough stick-spear missed its mark. Berries and nuts eased his hunger, but only temporarily. As much as he longed to stay with his furred friends, he'd need to get a job. He could do odd jobs like mucking out stalls or mowing lawns, but who would hire someone not yet thirteen? He'd have to lie about his age and completely recreate his identity, or risk being returned to his uncle.

High above, a dark bird flew free as the sky, its red-brown wings spanning out as if in joyous celebration. A falcon, Dominic realized, admiring the beauty and grace of the bird and longing to fly free, too. It would be so wonderful if he—

A sharp blast exploded.

The majestic falcon dropped like stone.

"NO!" Dominic cried, taking off running.

Visions of gun-toting poachers fueled Dominic's anger and pushed him to run faster. As he neared a meadow, he spotted a middle-aged man, outfitted in camouflage, pointing a shiny rifle skyward. The hunter took one look at Dominic, whose hard-boiled anger exploded with each pounding footstep, and blanched like he was scared enough to wet his pants. He fled in the opposite direction.

Ignoring the man, Dominic kept going—and a short

while later he found the falcon. The tangle of feathers lay in a dense thicket of brush, unmoving. Dominic's heart sank as if he'd been shot, too. A wind-blown creature flying free one moment, then gone in a blast of stupidity.

"Goddamned hunter," Dominic swore.

There was nothing he could do, so he turned to leave—but then heard a faint wing flutter. With a start, he turned back. Taking off his shirt and wrapping it around his hand for protection, he carefully picked tangled branches away from the bird. Dominic gently lifted up the near-dead creature, joyful to feel a faint pulse of life—there was no blood or bullet hole, only ripped tail features. But the bird was limp, probably stunned by the blast.

For hours, Dominic kept the bird warm, rewarded at last by a flutter of wings and opening eyes. The bird started to panic at the restricting shirt around his feathers, but Dominic instinctively cast out a mental message of trust and safety, just as he had done with Volcano. To his amazement, this calmed the bird. And by that nightfall, boy and bird shared a deep bond, which is how Dominic knew it was time to let go.

The falcon spread its wings, rising into the sky and disappearing in one sharp screech of good-bye. Staring at the empty sky, Dominic thought about his mother, about Volcano, and now about the falcon: all gone.

He was completely alone.

*   *   *

The next morning brought rain and chills worse than anything he'd ever experienced. Dominic's skin burned, yet he shivered from cold. He couldn't think clearly, and wanted only to return to his wooded childhood home. But he couldn't—even fevered, he knew this was impossible. All that was left was Uncle Jim's ramshackle house.

He would never go back there.

The woods, which had seemed friendly, now poked and shoved and pushed him away. He couldn't find food and hunger gnawed him painfully. He kept on walking, imagining once that he saw his mother waving at him, beckoning him to follow her on a trail. But the vision faded and the trail dead-ended at a paved road. Feverish chills gripped him and he collapsed to the ground, wrapping his arms around his burning skin.

He didn't even hear the car until the blue and red lights were flashing around him. He couldn't resist, and sagged into the arms that lifted him. A blanket was wrapped around his shivering shoulders, and he was bundled into a police car.

Sick, beyond rational thought, he felt the world spiral into blackness.

When he opened his eyes, Dominic hoped this was a bad dream. But the cot and diesel smells were real. He was back at Uncle Jim's.

It was no surprise that the door was locked.

He kicked and pounded, but the door remained a

sturdy jailer. There was nothing else to do but sink back into sleep … and hope to never wake up.

*　　　*　　　*

His mother's ebony eyes regarded him lovingly as she looked at him.

"Fight, Nicky," she said, in that soft voice he'd almost forgotten and now missed with an ache worse than hunger. "I'm sorry I couldn't protect you. I thought my brother would care for you, but I was wrong."

"I hate him." Dominic snapped up on the cot, not sure whether he was speaking to a ghost or a memory.

"Hate destroys all that is good."

"Nothing is good anymore. I tried to get away and look where I am again. Only this time I don't even have Volcano."

"You did a good thing for your dog, but now you need to take care of yourself. Hurry and leave before it's too late." Her voice rose with urgency. "Hurry!"

There was a jingle of keys, causing Dominic to jerk his head toward the door. When he looked back for his mother, she was gone. But the door was opening, filling with the large-boned, scowling face of Uncle Jim.

"You're awake?" he snorted.

Dominic glared.

"Stupid little bastard, where the hell is my dog?"

Dominic pursed his lips tightly.

Uncle Jim stomped over to the cot and grabbed Dominic by the shoulder. "Speak to me when I talk to you, boy. I asked where you hid my dog."

Still Dominic said nothing.

The brutal hand across his head sent him reeling backward, rolling off the cot and falling dazed onto the floor. Already weakened from fever, Dominic couldn't even lift his hand to cover his face when the second round came. Pain was almost a friend by now, its blackness sending him away.

When he awoke again, rain was falling, soaking his clothes and dripping into his parched mouth. He was lying on the ground, outside by the dog house, trapped by a long chain to the same metal stake that had trapped Volcano. A steel shackle circled his ankle, the attached chain only allowing him to move a few feet in any direction. The only thing within his reach was a bowl of dog food.

A glance toward the driveway showed that his uncle's car was gone, but the taunting words stayed behind: "You stole my dog, so take his place. You're my dog now."

At least his fever was gone, Dominic thought, with a small sense of relief. His thoughts were clearer, too, and he remembered the dream about his mother. It felt so real, as if she'd been there trying to protect him. She'd wanted him to leave—only her warning came too late. How could he leave now, with a shackle trapping him like a dog? And what would happen when his uncle returned? Would he be forgiven and released—or suffer more beatings?

Fight back, he could hear his mother saying.

But to fight, he'd need to gain strength.

"I won't eat dog food," he swore.

The rain stopped, replaced by sun that burned his skin and made him thirsty. He found rainwater in a dirt-crusted dish. As he drank, both disgusted and refreshed, he tried to think of a way out. But there was none. His uncle would never let him go, not unless he gave Volcano's location away...which he'd never do.

That evening, his uncle returned and pointed to the dog dish.

"Not hungry?" Uncle Jim snorted. "Get used to dog food, unless you're ready to tell me where that mutt of mine is."

Dominic turned away.

"Fine. Let's see how you hold out for one more day."

Then Uncle Jim went inside the house and didn't come out until he left for work the next morning.

Dominic stared at the dog food, which now resembled mud soup. He was so hungry, he could eat mud—but not dog food. The indignity of it would be a defeat far worse than hunger. How long could he hold out?

Hours later, as he came close to giving in, he heard a shrill shriek above him. Looking up, he saw red-brown feathers, and a sharp beak curved around something silvery.

When the falcon dropped the fish into Dominic's lap, he thought he must be dreaming. But the fish was wet and real and the first solid food he'd had in days.

"Thank you," he told the bird, who was already flying away.

A few hours later the bird returned, with something pulpy and bloody that reminded Dominic of road kill. Yet it was a gift, and he was hungry.

When Uncle Jim returned home that night to find the dog food still in the dish, he swore and stomped over to Dominic. His fist flew, but Dominic refused to cry out. Instead, he focused on the damp earth where he'd buried the food's bones, smiling secretly to himself, flying in his mind on red-brown wings.

The next day, sultry sun shifted into warm rain. Even with visits from the bird (whom Dominic had named Dagger because of the way he dove to the ground, slicing the sky with sharp knife-claws), the damp discomfort of being chained had weakened him. Dominic doubted he could last much longer like this, and wondered if letting go, to be with his mother, was the only way out.

But hope returned when he saw that the metal post holding his chain in place could wiggle. The combination of soggy ground and his continued tugging at it was loosening the post. If he could just lift it, the chain would slip off to freedom.

While he gnawed on a fish, feeling more animal than human, he kept working at the post. Back and forth, back and forth, pushing, pulling. Thinking of beatings and the blood on Volcano's fur, Dominic gave the post a vicious shove—and it twisted out of the ground.

After days of exposure, abuse, and chains, he could

leave the yard. And once he was inside the house, he'd find tools to cut the shackle.

The chain dragged behind his foot as he started toward the house—but a sudden noise stopped him. The familiar grind and rumble of his uncle's car. Damn! Why now, when he was so close? With the chain still on his ankle, he couldn't outrun his uncle.

But he could fool him—he could pretend to still be chained to the post, then escape later. Quickly, he shoved the steel post back into the ground, careful not to topple it. Then he settled back on the ground, his head hung down like the sorry dog he was supposed to be.

His uncle kicked at the untouched dog dish. "Stupid boy, why don't you eat?" he demanded. "You'd rather starve?"

"As if you care," he muttered, staying close to the post and hoping his uncle didn't notice the telltale lean.

"When I get my dog back, I'll let you go, even let you sleep and eat in the house."

"I don't know where he is," Dominic said.

"Liar!" His uncle reared back with his hand, ready to strike, when a sharp cry from overhead caught his attention.

Dominic glanced up at red-tipped wings and a beak full of fish. Not now! he thought, sending a message for Dagger to go away. But the falcon had already opened its beak, and a silvery fish plopped at Dominic's feet.

"What the crap?" Uncle Jim bellowed. He looked up at the bird, then down at the fish. "What kind of freaky bird feeds people?"

Dominic backed up, stopping only when he noticed the stake that once confined him slipping sideways. He moved closer, grasping it to hold it in place.

"Damned bird ain't natural. I'll take care of it for good," Uncle Jim said angrily. He rushed into the house and came out moments later with a rifle.

"NO!" Dominic shouted. "You can't shoot him!"

"Can't I?" Uncle Jim lifted the gun, his teeth gleaming in an ugly smile as he released the safety. "Just watch. Then I'll get my whip and take care of you."

Dominic shouted again, jerking the chain so that the post flew out of the soggy ground. Uncle Jim turned angrily, lowering the gun so that instead of pointing at the bird, it was aimed at Dominic. A sadistic sneer carved hatred on the older man's face. His trigger finger moved.

Dominic moved faster. He reached down and grabbed the long chain dangling from his ankle, then flung it like a whip. The chain lashed out at his uncle's face. The rifle fell from Uncle Jim's fingers, and he cried out as the chain wrapped around his neck like a metal snake. As he reeled backward, his head made an awful cracking sound and he fell to the ground, his neck twisted at an odd angle.

Dominic stared for several long seconds, certain his uncle was dead. He had no doubt his uncle would have shot him with no remorse. He'd acted in self defense, saving the bird, saving himself. But who would believe him?

He cut off his shackles, packed a bag, and placed an anonymous call to 911.

Then he shut the door behind him as he walked into a new life, with a new name, in a new place. High above, in the sky, a red-winged bird soared.

Only when he was miles away did he pull out a small paper from his pocket.

Reading the address where Volcano now lived in peace, Dominic considered going there—then decided to wait. Dominic-the-Boy wanted a family, but Dominic-the-Man knew he had to make it on his own. Then he could seek out old friends.

The woman in the wide hat had told him that they would meet again.

Yes, they would.

Someday.

The Beginning